RAGE

J Carrell Jones

Mythical Legends Publishing

RAGE is a work of fiction. The characters, incidents, and dialogs are products of the author's imagination and are not to be construed as real. Any resemblance to actual events or persons, living or dead, is entirely coincidental.

A Mythical Legends Publishing Mass-Market Edition

ISBN-13: **978-1-943958-69-6**

Printed in the United States of America

9 8 7 6 5 4 3 2

RAGE

J CARRELL JONES

Icarus' Flight

Mary, the flight attendant, smiled as she walked passed me. Like the others, she was slim with dark hair. She had a natural way about herself and smiled easily. Earlier, she had brought me a Gin and Tonic with Peanuts. We made small talk until she mentioned her sister served in Iraq - the first invasion. We had something in common and an instant bond formed. She worked the aisles and every now and then she made her way to my side. Eye contact was always intense. We smiled, with both of us licking our lips. She'd shift her gaze and would move on. Our little game together.

Then . . . he walked by. I first saw him at the ticket gate. He looked normal enough, but there was something off about him. He was handsome, tall, toned. Grunge seemed to be his choice in clothing. Today, it seemed more so. I watched him when he handed his passport to the ticket agent. They chatted, she even laughed. So, why was I put on edge? His eyes. They were . . . not right. He had been high on something and was just starting to come off it. I would have guessed Meth. He was probably starting to tweak. So, when he walked by me I took noticed. He stepped into an unoccupied lavatory. The pilot had just turned off the fasten seatbelt sign several minutes ago and the cabin stirred to life. Mary walked by and asked if I needed anything. I said, "Yes . . ."

She smiled and said "absolutely." She came in close and whispered, "Once midway over the Atlantic things will be very quiet." She then stood up, "Another Gin and Tonic?"

I returned the smile. "Yes, please. Thank you."

She got an order from the guy next to me. When she left, he leaned over to me and whispered, "Lucky you."

I laughed, "She makes a great Gin and Tonic."

He laughed too. He started to say something when . . . it happened.

We heard a roar behind us. It was extreme and primal. Grunge yelled, "I got to get out!' He was naked and his face was scrunched up demonically.

A woman turned to move out of his way. He grabbed her hair and pulled hard toward him. His teeth bit deep into her scalp. She screamed as he broke bone. Another passenger punched him in the face. Grunge released the woman and fell back. He got up and pounced on the man. Teeth sank into his neck and blood squirted everywhere. I undid my seatbelt and jumped out into the aisle. I spotted a laptop and grabbed it. I remembered saying, "May I" as I lifted the laptop over my head and came down hard on Grunge's Skull. He yelled louder, dropped the man and came after me. I kicked him in the chest hard enough to break brick. He brushed the kick off and back handed me. The laptop took most of the force. He ran over me and headed for the cockpit. A Flight Attendant tried to stop him. He raged harder, hit her in the shoulder. She screamed as her collarbone snapped. He crashed into the door screaming. The door held for several moments, then caved in. Someone yelled, "What the . . . get out!"

I stepped back out into the aisle and headed toward Grunge. I could see him swinging at the Pilot and Co-pilot. Then . . . three shots and Grunge raged more. Someone screamed and the plane banked sharply. The navigator swung and hit him in the head. Grunge swung back hard and I heard a deep sounding crack. Another shot and Grunge came out dragging the Navigator. His body was limp. I was about to hit him in the head again when the Air Marshal appeared. He ran up to Grunge, jabbed a small Stun Gun in his neck and sparked the device. Grunge tossed the Navigator aside. He swung and connected with the Marshal's right arm. The Stun gun, released, hit the side wall. Grunge punched the Marshal in the Jaw, breaking it. The Marshal spit a dozen teeth out and reached for something in his jacket pocket. Grunge kicked him in the chest. The Marshal fell back, but true to his training he had his gun out with his left hand and double tapped. Grunge stopped cold as both bullets hit him between the eyes.

I reached the Marshal. He fainted. "Flight Attendant!" I snapped. One came up and cradled the Marshal's head between her legs. I got up and stared at a lifeless Grunge now. Blood soaked the carpet from the gaping wound at the back of his head. The plane banked sharply again, dropped some, then leveled out. I ran to the cockpit. Blood was nearly everywhere. An unconscious Captain had deep scratch marks over his face. I could tell his right eye was a lost cause. The Co-pilot was slouched over the wheel. His left shoulder dislocated and the right arm was broken at the forearm. I yelled, "We need some help in here! Is there anyone with medical training?" Mary appeared with several people. A middle-aged woman and two younger men.

The woman said, "I'm a GP."

The two guys where both Med students. One in his first year, the second graduating soon.

We eased the Captain out of his chair and into the aisle. Grunge had been dragged out of the way by some of the passengers. The Co-pilot refused to leave.

I pulled out my ID, "United Nation's Agent Bechard," and sat in the Pilot's seat.

The Co-pilot said, "I can't leave my post. I have to land this thing."

I replied, "How? One dislocated shoulder and a broken arm."

He winced in pain, "Then sit there and help me fly this bird."

I nodded and buckled myself in.

One of the Med students secured the Co-pilot's arm to his side. Before that, he discovered broken ribs. He set the broken arm before splinting it. The Co-pilot said, "My bag. Over there. I have ibuprofen in there."

Mary had a cup of water already in hand. The Med student, Patrick, held the bottle. He gave the Co-pilot eight 200 mg tablets.

The Co-pilot washed them down with the water. After a few moments he said, "Damn maniac! What the devil was he on?"

I shrugged. "I thought he was coming off a meth high before take-off, but this rage is nothing like a tweak."

He winced and straightened himself up. He checked the instrumentation and fumbled putting the headset on. Mary helped.

I put the Captain's on.

Mary had a sorrowful expression. I looked her way and gave a lopsided smile. Her features softened. She said, "Ms. Bechard . . ."

"Please call me Karen . . ."

"Karen, can I get you anything? Coffee, tea . . ."

I let the pause linger some seconds, smiled and said, "Coffee would be great."

She smiled my way, turned, saw the blot of blood, frowned and headed toward the back. From my vantage point I could see most of business class was empty of live passengers. It was now the morgue. Grunge and two other bodies were seated with blankets over them. One flight attendant was standing near crying.

The Co-pilot communicated to LaGuardia that we had a situation. He looked beaten. Figuratively and literally.

I was staring ahead when the Co-pilot asked, "Miss, Karen, right?"

"Yeah," I said.

"Call me Martin."

"Okay, Martin. How are you feeling?"

"Like shit. Bastard."

I nodded.

"I ain't never seen anything like this. hold . . ."

LaGuardia Tower gave Martin a frequency and heading.

He responded, "LaGuardia, Delta zero-niner-zero-niner, starting turn in a few. How's traffic?"

"Delta 0909, traffic has been diverted. The sky is yours. Move to 220."

He placed his hand over the mike, "Karen, that softkey off-center . . ."

I hovered my finger over the display screen.

He nodded, "Yeah, that one. Press."

I did.

"Turn that knob over there to 220." He

puckered his lips to a knob.

"Piney, huh?"

He chuckled. "Yeah, thirteen years now."

I turned the knob until 220 displayed on my front screen.

He reached over with his right arm and pressed several buttons.

The plane turned on its own.

He spoke in his mike again. "LaGuardia 220."

LaGuardia answered and gave him several more questions. He answered. Finished and sat back.

Mary entered with a tray. A coffee pot, cup, sugar, cream, and pastry were on it.

I said, "one sugar no cream, please," and took a pastry.

"We have a few minutes before landing . . ." He paused a long time and finally said, "I'm not sure I'll make it. I feel really bad."

"Of course, you'll make it." I hoped.

"You're gonna have to land this plane. I'm feeling really, really bad. I might pass out on you."

"Mary," I said, "Get the Doctor."

A moment later our GP showed up. She looked into the Co-Pilot's eyes and said, "He hit you in the head pretty hard didn't he?"

The Co-pilot nodded. "I just want . . ." He never finished. He slumped into the Doctor's arms. She called to the Med Students. They carried him out.

I thought, 'Well, Uck. We're doomed.'

Mary stood there for a moment. Tears welled up in her eyes. Without me asking she slipped into the Co-pilot's seat. This one has got to be a keeper I thought. Her bottom lip quivered as she buckled in and placed the headset on. She gave me a weak smile.

I smiled back and switched on the mike. "LaGuardia, this is Delta zero-niner-zero-niner. United Nation Agent Karen Bechard speaking. We have a situation."

Mary looked over at me with mixed emotions - surprise, shock, disbelief, and relief.

The Tower answered, "Delta zero-niner-zero-niner, what's the situation?"

"Co-pilot is out. I'm sitting Pilot seat and Flight Attendant Mary . . ." I placed my hand over the mike.

She replied, "Hernandez."

". . . Hernandez in Co-pilot seat. Delta zero-niner-zero-niner out."

There was a long pause. Then, "Delta zero-niner-zero-niner, we see you holding course. Do you have flight experience?"

I answered, "Some. Apache copter, Huey, twin turbine four passengers, glider."

"All Planes, this is LaGuardia tower, secure for emergency landing. Delta 0909 can you locate the Captain's Radio Tuning control? Underneath and left of the engine throttles. Turn to frequency 121.65."

I found the control and made the change. Mary did the same thing on her side.

"Tower, both Pilot and Co-pilot radios are at frequency 121.65."

"Ms. Bechard, you're moving away from us. We have to turn you around."

"Tower, call me Karen. I'm ready. Instruct away."

"Okay Karen, we need to first run through a few things. The altimeter is just left of center."

I replied, "It's the bottom of the three gauges. Airspeed is center."

"Correct. What is your speed?"

I said, "270 knots per second."

There was a pause. "Okay, we need to slow you down a bit. But first I need you to start making an approach for landing. I read you at 25,000 feet. We need you at 10,000 and aimed back at us."

I looked over to Mary. She was studying the controls. The flight manual was in her lap and opened. She was power reading.

One of the other flight attendants came into the cabin. "Anything I can do?"

Mary said, "Hey, Liz. I'd love a drink but coffee would be best. Can you warm up Karen's coffee, please?"

Liz stood there for a while, not knowing what to say or do. Mary noticed, looked up, and said, "Liz, no worries. Karen has some flight experience and LaGuardia is walking us through the basics now. We'll be safe on the ground soon."

Liz touched Mary on the shoulder. I think she wanted to give her a hug, but left instead with my cup.

I closed the mike and said, "Mary?"

She looked up and over to me.

"Dinner then my place?"

She smiled and moved a bunch of hair behind her ear. "Any restaurant?"

Tower was talking in my ear. I mouthed, "of course," and focused what Tower had to say. Mary and I worked together. We ran down the descent checklist quickly and started working on approach. Tower had us turned around and minutes within the airport. The weather turned from nice to crappy all in an hour.

Tower said, "Karen, you got wind at South East . . ." He paused.

Wind. Great. Even experienced pilots can find it challenging.

I replied, "And I thought this was supposed to be a tough landing."

Mary hit the fasten seatbelt sign and toggled the cabin intercom on. "Ladies and Gentlemen. We are starting our approach now. Please take your seats and fasten your seat belts. If you haven't done so, please place your tray tables in their upright position. Make sure all loose items are stowed properly. Flight Attendants, please secure cabin for landing." She toggled the intercom off and let out a long breath.

"Delta 0909 is ready for instructions," I said. "Talk us through."

Tower said we were going to do a Sideslip. The runway was still dry so that was one less thing to worry about.

We started our descent.

Mary toggled intercom. "Prepare for descent."

We gave each other one last look. I took a deep breath and pulled back on the throttle. Mary dropped the landing gear and I moved the flaps to 25. The plane descended smoothly. I could make out 22 at the front of the runway. Tower instructed me to adjust rudder and ailerons. I pulled further back on the throttle further dropping our speed. I've landed turboprops in crosswinds but doing so in such a huge craft so high off the ground made for a different experience. To my right I saw the centerline of the runway. In front of me was Flushing Bay. I could see the 678 backing up. Then the plane tilted. Tower instructed me to drop my left wing down a bit. I did and nearly touched ground. I jerked back and the plane tilted crazily to the right. Tower calmly said don't power steer. Imagine you have an egg sitting on top of the steering wheel and try not to drop it. I turned in and the plane adjusted. The runway came up fast and just before the wheels touched Tower said re-adjust and point the nose centerline. I felt the rear tires contact ground first. As instructed, I dropped the nose down and felt the hard hit of the tires. Mary set the spoilers to up. I engaged thrust reverse. I watched the speed go from 150 knots to 80 knots to 50. I hit the brakes and thought screw the taxi. This plane is stopping now. Some seconds later our 747 came to rest. Mary quickly went through turning everything off. I found the APU Gen 1 and Gen 2 switches. We had power. In the background, I heard applauds. I was happy to have dodged this bullet and not made a debris path. Mary and I unbuckled. I stepped out and couldn't believe what I saw. In the moment, Grunge had knocked me down and ran to the cockpit he ripped several seats to shreds. One armrest was bent out at an odd angle. What was disturbing was the blood splatters. On the windows, the floor, and the seats. The first three rows of business had been vacated. I told Mary I had to go and make a report. She said she would, hopefully, be at the Airport Hilton. We touched hands briefly and I took the nearest emergency exit slide. Mary stayed to help evacuate the plane. I made a mental note: Karen, keep this one happy and talk to Vadnez about making her an agent.

Having Issues

Vadnez sat behind a rather large oak desk. His monitor was off-centered and a picture of his wife and kids to its right. The desk was polished clean. Neat stacks of reports were to the left of the monitor. He had three pencils of the same length next to the reports. The man was so fastidious I wondered if his wife and kids wondered how hard it would be to hide the body. He was reading my report. After turning a few more papers he looked up. "Ms. Bechard, you really should use more active sentences."

I nodded and waited.

He closed the folder. "Interesting. The local coroner thinks he was on A-PPV."

I whispered, "Bath Salt."

Vadnez said, "You may not know this, but A-PPV's street name is Bath Salt." He looked at me.

That was my que. "Oh really? I hadn't known."

"Ms. Bechard, research, research, research. How you are one of my most efficient and effective agents is beyond me."

I said, "Luck and Karma. I kiss lots of babies and puppies."

He stared at me for a long while.

I stared back. No one can out stare me. Not even Vadnez. He's tried many times - and failed just as many times.

He cleared his throat and broke the stare.

Ha! I win again I thought and forced myself not to smile.

"This problem is becoming an international issue."

I nodded.

He grabbed the top folder and handed it to me. "Your new assignment."

On the cover was a picture of a female scientist. She looked pretty and wore wire rim round lens glasses. Her hair was light brown, her skin was sun deprived pale. She looked 30something. I looked up.

"Dr. Dorothy Reanders, super genius. IQ well over 200. Her first PH.D was at 12." He paused.

I could still put a bullet through her head and

she'd be dead. Being a Wyle E. Coyote did not impress me. She was probably an arrogant bitch who would whine and moan if things didn't go her way. I just replied, "Oh, really?"

Vadnez smiled. He figured he had my attention. Such an easy study. "I would like you to interview her."

"Does she know she is on our radar?"

"She is not a suspect, Ms. Bechard. Ms. Hill is on another assignment. Otherwise she would be doing the interview."

I nodded. Katherine "kitty" Hill was cool. I liked her. She was good at pulling info from folks. "Reanders is not a suspect."

He nodded. "We just need information on a growing problem. She is an expert on drug influenced behavior. This particular Bath Salt may be a new variant. Dr. Reanders can help us confirm this."

I nodded.

"She is also on retainer to the UN."

Ah, the point. We retained her for her brains and I'm not supposed to piss her off. But, I thought, then don't send me. Pissing people off is what I do best.

"Understood, sir."

Vadnez smiled. He liked it when I said 'sir.'

I collected my things and left. It was this side of 1:00 pm and I was hungry. The Unicef House Cafeteria was still open. They had a new turkey sandwich on the menu and I was dying to try it. The pictures on the menu looked good and Chef Schembeck and staff would never uck up a sandwich. After getting the sandwich I found an empty booth and sat. I allowed myself several delicious bites before I opened Reanders' folder.

She had a dozen scholarly awards, inventions, and commendations - all before age twenty. She's on the Presidential Science Advisory Council and has consulted for NASA and ESA. With each page on Reanders the feeling of 'cold clinical time bomb' increased. Dr. Dorothy Reanders, super-genius: Cold, calculating, sociopath. In her youth, her inventions were about saving and enhancing the quality of human life. At 16 years old, she focused on enhancing personal comfort. At eighteen it was about self-indulging. At twenty she focused on building her fortune. She made billions from the stock market and gave not one penny to any charitable organization. She voted Independent, rejected all mono-thesis religions. I couldn't tell if she was spiritual, just not right-winged, or completed alt-right. She had no close personal friends and rarely socialized. She declined most international speaking invitations. I should have admired her, but I didn't. Pity? Concern? Fear? Maybe all of the above. I've met folks with a third her IQ quite dangerous. What would I do if she turned out to be a bad guy? I closed the folder and finished my sandwich. I had a date with a spooky-genius. Time for my A-game.

I reached Dr. Reanders' office by five. Some eye-candy was at the receptionist desk. He looked up.

"May I help you?"

Total gay. He was beefcake and tall, dark eyes with a 5 o'clock shadow. Nice lips and straight short cut black hair. Such a waste. I'd love to have road driven him to exhaustion. I smiled. "Yes, please. Karen Bechard, UN Agent. Here to see Dr. Reanders."

He looked over to a clipboard. "Oh yes. Right here. The Doctor said to hold your appointment off a bit if you came early. She's on a call to a Governor right now."

A Governor. I gave him a slight smile and glided my eyes over what I could see of him.

"Would you like some coffee while you wait? Water maybe?"

I said, "Coffee would be nice, thank you. No cream, one pack of Splenda if you have any."

He got up and I watched him as he walked past and down a short hall. His arms were huge and well defined. The Brachii on both arms were thick and snaked nicely down the biceps' length. I would very much be his bottom.

"Here you go Miss Bechard. I added some cookies."

I took the coffee and cookies. "Thank you . . .?"

"Guy."

"You certainly are, Guy."

He laughed and smiled sweetly. On him it looked good. Please tell me you're Bi, I raunchily thought.

He sat down and started tapping away on his keyboard. Every now and then he would laugh. It would start out slow, like he was looking at something dirty and didn't want anyone to know, then it would increase in volume and intensity. He was a man who loved to laugh and laughed often.

I looked around the office. It was pleasing to the eyes. Several huge paintings adorned the walls. Reanders was into African and Islander motif. On that I agreed. I could like her about one thing at least. A few minutes later, Guy's phone rang.

"Guy, speaking . . . she is . . . yes . . . yes . . . very much so . . . " He casually looked over my way.

I acted like I didn't notice.

He continued, "No . . . not at the moment . . . okay . . . " He started tapping on his keyboard. "You got it? . . . five minutes. . . okay." He hung up. And tapped away again on his keyboard. A minute later I heard his dirty little laugh. A minute after that he looked over to me. "Dr. Reanders will be down in a few minutes to see you."

I nodded and said, "Facebook?"

He laughed and said, "How'd you know?"

I smiled back, "I'd be doing it too if I wasn't here."

He leaned forward, "Did you see the one about giving a shit?"

I laughed, "That was a good one."

A few seconds later the door opened. Reanders stood in the doorway pissed. I made a mental note: very possessive about her's. She was dressed in a long white lab coat. Underneath that was a grey pants suit. Her blouse was white. Her hair was pulled back in a bun and she wore the same metal round rim glasses I saw in the photo. She stared hard and frowned.

I stood up and reach my hand out. "Dr. Reanders, I am Karen Bechard, UN Agent."

She stared at my hand for a moment, then looked at Guy. He moved his face behind his monitor. I kept my hand out, daring her not to accept it.

Nearly a minute went by before she slightly grabbed it and shook once. I wasn't sure if that was a battle won for me or for her.

"Miss Bechard, my time is limited. How long will this take?"

"As long as it takes."

She stared me in the eyes and I nearly blinked first. Guy coughed and Reanders broke the stare first. "Yes?"

"You have another appointment in 30 minutes. Mr. Chen from ZenTech."

Reanders nodded. "Follow me into the small conference room." She turned and walked to the far end on the office and entered a small room. I saw a small table at the center of four chairs. She took one I took the opposite.

"Thank you for the Inter . . . "

"Can we get on with this?" She said.

I paused and counted to 10 - in my head. "You had a chance to read the preliminary toxicology report?"

She yawned., "Yeah, all standard stuff."

I waited for more. "And?"

She looked bored. "And what?"

"I'd like a little more than 'standard stuff' please."

She sized me up. "Was it your father or mother?"

"Pardon?"

"Which one was black?"

Now that was from left field. "What does that have to … "

"It was your father. I see Asian, too. Philippines or Polynesian. That would be your Mother … "

"Dr. Reanders, please, can we stick … "

She slammed her hand down hard on the table and yelled, "Don't interrupt me when I'm talking."

That took me by surprise.

She continued, "The male subject had a cocktail of ingredients in his blood. A-PPV, Cannabis, caffeine … most interesting this." She paused and thought for a few seconds. "He had been drinking the night before. Couldn't tell what, but it was at least 40 proof. Then he smoked marijuana followed by Bath Salts. Meth came later. He was probably coming off a Meth high before take-off . . ."

"He had . . ."

"What did I say about . . . "

"I was there! I was on that flight!"

She reflected and changed her demeanor. "Really? How did he act just before?"

"What?"

"It's a simple question. It doesn't require much thought. You were a witness. I want to know his behavior moments before he raged."

I was so mad I wanted to slap her. I was right. Very arrogant bitch hijacking my interview.

She studied my face and smiled. "Miss Bechard, the UN is asking me for help. Why are you hampering my willingness to help?"

That was like cold water to my face. She leaned back and smirked. That started to piss me off even more. All of 5 minutes she managed to control the interview. She jerked my emotions with surgical precision and that bothered me. So, I decided to play along and supply her with lots of rope. I leaned back as if I were defeated. "His eyes were off."

She cocked her head. "That is hardly scientific. More precise please."

"Dilated pupils, watery eyes, dull expression, but he was very conversational. Not agitated."

She thought about that. "And he wasn't aggressive until after the plane took off?"

I nodded. "He went into the lavatory. A few minutes after that he raged. I don't know if he removed his clothes before or after he came out. I heard him roar . . ."

"Roar?"

"Yeah, roared."

"Was he hypersexual?"

"What?"

"Pay attention, please. Did he try and rape anyone?"

"No, just completely and totally angry. He first bit into a woman's skull and cracked bone. One of the passengers gave him a pretty good hit to the head. He brushed it off and broke his neck with a punch."

A long moment she closed her eyes. Minutes went by, then, "It's the . . . What else?"

"He withstood a 1,000,000 volt stun to the neck and several shots in the torso. The bullets to the brain stopped him."

"It's a variant."

I just looked at her.

"It a variant of the A-PPV substance. The Meth and cannabis negated each other - interesting. I'll have to think about that one, but the rage was not from him coming off the Meth. I noticed an increased level of islet beta-cells. The subject's glucose levels, before death, topped 600. His pancreas and liver went into overdrive. Fascinating . . . his liver was secreting large amounts of glucose and the pancreas was pumping large amounts of insulin. That probably drove his core temperature up. There were high levels of epinephrine in his bloodstream. That makes sense. What I find disturbing is his testosterone levels were normal. Someone with that much rage should have elevated levels. I would have to check for monoamine oxidase deficiency. I didn't see a report on metal levels, but I would bet the subject had low levels of zinc in his brain. Copper level would probably be high . . ."

I pretty much followed her. I let her ramble a few more minutes, but I got what I came for. She talked as if she were comparing what happened to what she thought should have happened. "Can this happen again." I interrupted.

She scowled intensively, "What did I tell you about inter . . ."

I did it again, "Can this happen again. Yes or no?"

Her cheeks turned red and she snatched the

folder I was holding. She angrily waved it in my face and yelled, "Haven't you been paying attention! Of course this can happen again. It's a variant. A manufactured drug! My goodness! How stupid can you be. A variant like this can tip the scale . . ." She stopped and placed the folder back on the table. She did not apologize for taking it in the first place.

Now it was my turn. She reached the edge but pulled herself back. I was going to bring her forward again and watch the fall. "Top or bottom?"

"What?"

"Please pay attention, top or bottom?"

"What kind of question is th . . ."

"You like it from behind don't you."

The light bulb came on and she realized what I was talking about. "That is none of your . . ."

"It's a simple question. Yes or no? You like it from behind. You don't swallow, but you rub it on your face."

She tried to slap me. I easily caught her hand and squeezed.

"Stop it. That hurts."

"You are a silly arrogant bitch. You have issues . . ."

"How dare . . ."

I squeezed tighter and she nearly cried. "I think you have something to do with this variant."

I watched her face closely and caught her first expression - guilt.

She recovered quickly but not fast enough. She yanked her hand away. "Don't come in here Goose-stepping. I'm an American citizen. You've no authority over me and I resent your pathetic attempt at bullying. Get the fuck out of my office, Chick!"

Suddenly, the door opened and Guy stepped in. "Dr. Reanders is everything okay?"

Dr. Reanders tried to stare me down. I was ready this time and had the upper hand. I could kick her ass and she knew it. She broke first, in front of Guy, and that had to hurt.

She hissed, "Get out of my office before I call the po . . ."

"And what? No jurisdiction over me. For someone smart, you're pretty dumb."

She turned full red.

I stepped toward her and she backed away. The expression on her face was totally priceless. She stormed out of the conference room and out into the main hallway. Doors slammed as she went further into her domain. Guy looked at me and sweetly smiled.

He said, "She can be such a bitch sometimes. Looks like it'll be high drama around here, but it was worth seeing it." And he did that dirty little laugh of his.

I took the crushed folder and walked out. It only took me a minute to reach my car. I feed the auto-parking meter my credit card and paid for the time I had parked. Just as I turned on to the main street my cell phone rang - my unlisted cell phone. The caller id was blank, which I didn't think possible. I let it ring a few times and answered.

"You've made me very angry you cunt." The call ended.

I thought the voice sounded like Reanders. A minute later my cell rang again. The caller id read, "Arrogant Bitch".

I answered, "Dr. Reanders?"

"I am very upset with you."

I looked at the phone for a second then placed it back to my ear. "And I'm supposed to what?"

"Is your real name Karen Bechard? Or is it Paula Haggard? Or Linda Holt?"

I could play that game too. "Dorothy . . ."

"You are not allowed to call me by my first name, Mutt."

Mutt? Now she was getting personal. "Hang

up now and I'll forget you called me names."

"Mutt, you crossed the line . . ."

"You know you are talking to a UN representative . . ."

"I'm talking to nothing. You invade my space and bully me. . . "

I ended the call and dialed Vadnez. This just got out of hand. The phone rang once then dropped. I pulled over and dug out my "official" mobile. It rang once and dropped. The signal was at full strength for both phones. Just them both phones rang. I answered one.

"You've embarrassed me and that is unforgiveable. . ."

I yelled, "You're a nut job!"

There was a long pause, then, "the streetlight in front of you is green. It'll change from green to yellow to green again."

I looked up and saw the light she was talking about. It indeed did change from green to yellow back to green. The realization I was in over my head was starting to sink in. Karen I told myself, 'you pissed off a spooky-genius. Be afraid.'

I could tell she was speaking with clenched teeth, "I . . . am . . . going . . . to . . . teach . . . you . . . a . . . lesson . . . you . . . fuckin . . . Mutt! Never mess with me. Never!"

Damn! I thought. Am I supposed to fear for my life now? This turned unreal. I thought for a few minutes and decided to go back to Reanders' office. At one traffic stop the light turned from red to green back immediately to red. She was letting me know I was being watched. I tried calling Vadnez again. It rang once then dropped. Then I had a lucky break. I remembered a payphone on the corner of Amsterdam and W 133rd St. It was just on the W 133rd side of City Gourmet Deli & Grocery, a corner store and not too far from me. I drove without signaling, caught traffic and opted to park. I'd deal with the ticket later.

I walked about a quarter mile when I realized Reanders had tapped into the remote camera throughout the city. It was my luck that NYC hadn't installed many remotes on this end. I suppose she could find some business and home security cams and tap into them, but NYC is big.

After thirty minutes of walking I reached the Phone. It was in good condition. I dialed our hotline. I exhaled when I got a second and third ring. Cortez picked up.

"Cortez speaking."

"Agent KB031174. I got a sitch."

A few seconds later, "Vadnez thought you would call in. What's the scale."

Bastard I thought. He suspected Reanders all this time. "Off the chart. Mobiles out. Hey, is Kitty on assignment?"

"Vadnez gave her the rest of the week off. Anything imminent?"

"Only at me. I'm requesting watch over rogue. Legal taps if possible. And variant confirmed. Rogue could be the original."

"Will relay. KB, good flying, sucky landing."

"Hey, I'm here talkin' to ya. What more is needed?"

"Point. BTW. More reports like the plane."

My blood went cold. "No shit?"

"Yes shit. Twelve in the last hour. Nothing like Miami. All on the ground."

"Noted. Out." I hung the phone up. I flagged down a cab and made my way back to Reanders' office.

Guy was still at his desk. He looked up, "Miss Bechard. Reanders is currently in a meeting. She said you would return and to give you this folder."

It was thick, probably fifty pages. I took it and sat on the couch - in front of a fresh cup of coffee and cookies. I gave Guy a look.

He shrugged, "She can be scary accurate most times."

I nodded and opened the folder to the first

page. It was a copy of my birth certificate. The second page was a fake death certificate. It had today's date on it. The subsequent pages were a collection of photos of me from youth to now. She had various documents on me as well. Kindergarten to college to my Army days to working at the UN. Everything. My life in a folder. I felt violated and that pissed me off. Reanders, super-genius, pushed the wrong buttons. I was not pissed. I was livid. She thought to have me fear for my safety. She tried to intimidate me. The stupid bitch. How dare she invade and expose me so raw. I must have been scary looking.

Guy was on the phone. He said a few words and hung up. I turned on him so fast he barely stifled a shriek.

I was at his desk before he knew it. "Office. Where. Now!"

Guy was pale and had the deer in the headlights look. "Two doors down. It's the right one."

I stormed out the office and stumped my way to the second door. Reanders, super-genius, made a mistake. She miscalculated and now reckoning day was upon her. Reanders, super-genius. Wrong. Reanders, super-fool, super-idiot, super-dumbass, super-gonna-get-her-ass-kicked was more like it. I made it to the door and stopped. I wasn't so out of control that I would barge right in. That would have been dumb on my part. So far Reanders had been one step ahead. I looked around the hallway and spotted two corner cameras. Both were pointed at me. I came off my rage and my adrenaline level dropped. I turned the knob and the door opened smoothly. I let it open wide before I stepped in. A second door was about ten feet away. The floor leading up to the door was polished wood. A sofa was on the right side of the room. It looked well used. An oak desk was on the other side. It had a huge screen monitor on top. There were lots of books stacked at various heights around the desk.

I had some choices to make: Open the other door, leave, or investigate. I chose to investigate. I looked around and couldn't find any obvious signs of cameras. I spotted a book by one of the sofa legs. The cover looked familiar. As I picked up the book I realized the sofa was not for sleeping when working late at night. I delightfully thought maybe Guy was Bi. The book definitely looked well read. The spine was broken in. There were various thick crease spots along the spine that indicated most read areas. I opened the book to one of the areas. And giggled. I was right. Reanders liked it from behind. The book was the Kama-Sutra Illustrated.

Rage or rage not. Do not try.

I sat on her sofa, read, and giggled. It tickled me to think that maybe I'm derailing her plans. I could imagine her fuming because I hadn't walked through that second door looking to kick butt. I turned another page and read. A few minutes later Reanders came out of the second door. She hovered over me as I read. I looked up, smiled, and said, "Join me, look away, or fucking do something."

She stared at me for a few seconds. "Ms. Bechard, I want to show you something." Her emotions were in perfect check.

"I find your sofa quite comfortable. Does Guy ride you often on it?"

She paled.

"I know he's gay, but money is money. Do

you clench or suck him off as a reward?"

She was so mad that she started to shake. "I think we got off on the wrong foot. I'd like to apologize for my behavior."

I closed the book, got up, looked her in the eyes, and said, "Apology will tentatively be accepted when given."

She worked her mouth into different expressions. She finally said, "Very well." She reached her hand out in a handshake. I stared at it for nearly a minute and shook it once. It had some lotion on it. I still wasn't sure if I won that battle or not. "Please follow me into my lab. I have something to show you related to your questioning." She turned and started to walk.

I stood fast. "Tell me now."

She froze, turned, and said, "It's more data on the variant. Because of security reasons I can only reveal so much."

I wasn't convinced.

"Among other things it was supposed to be an endurance enhancer. If you want more follow me. If not, please leave."

I hesitated, then started to leave.

She blurted out, "Your boss called and reminded me of my contractual obligations."

I followed her through the second door into

a small chamber. It was more like a large closet. Towels hung on one side and a sink on the other. She stepped up to the sink and washed her hands. As she was drying them she thought for a second and said, "Sorry, old habits. It had nothing to do with the handshake. You probably should wash yours as well."

I did, but I started to feel warm. I looked over to Reanders. She was slowly drying her hands. My eyesight started to narrow. Reanders lend in close and said, "Miss. Bechard, you are not looking well. Is something the matter?"

I turned to choke her skinny little neck but couldn't hold onto the right one. A few seconds later I blacked out. 'I'm spanking your ass the first chance I get,' was my last thought.

I woke up in the middle of being tied to an old wooden chair. There were several men in lab coats standing around holding clipboards. Another two had just finished tying my waist to the chair. Amateurs. Not one could tie a decent knot.

Reanders had her back to me working at a nearby desk.

I surprised the two men and knocked their heads together. The other three froze. I flexed hard, grabbed the top few rope turns and lifted.

The entire wrap became slack. I reached out and grabbed Reanders by her bun.

She yelped "What the . . . "

I spun her around and gave her several hard slaps to the face. Then I lift her lab coat over her head and bent her over my knee. She dropped easily into place. In one motion I pulled her pants and panties down to her knees and spanked hard. Her ass was very soft and smooth. Immediately her cheeks turned red. She now had a dozen hand prints on both cheeks. I briefly enjoyed the view and I was about to give her another dozen when strong arms grabbed me.

Guy said, "I can't believe you let her do that to the Doctor."

Reanders tumbled off my knees and heavily landed on the floor.

She got up embarrassed. Her face cheeks were just as red as her butt cheeks. She slapped me as hard as she could.

I laughed. "Dorothy, you spend too much time in the lab and on your knees. The gym I say. The gym."

She hit me harder. I felt that one.

I said, "Better. Don't stop at the face. Follow through."

She did and the slap stung. She did it several

more times then she held her hand and rubbed the center of her palm with the other hand.

"Not used to beating people up, I see."

"Will someone shut this bitch up?"

One of the males gagged me with a cloth. Guy instructed the others on how to tie a knot. Within minutes my arms, legs, chest, and hands were tied to the chair.

Reanders had composed herself and went back to her desk. She walked over to a small refrigerator on one of the workbenches. "You know, Ms. Bechard. You should consider yourself lucky. You'll be the first Human to test this out." She had a metal canister in her hands. She slowly opened the top and poured a glowing light blue liquid into a glass beaker. She recapped the container and placed it backed into the refrigerator. She carefully placed the beaker on the table and slid some thick gloves over each hand. "This is not scientific, but you know what? I don't care. I hate you so much I hope this mixture is a failure and kills you."

I tried to escape, but the knots were too good.

"At best, you'll feel euphoric before pain hits, but you'll have an incredible amount of strength and endurance for hours. At worst you'll die in horrible pain." She picked up a remote and pressed a button. I was hit with high voltage.

"If you struggle again I'll fry you. Try to escape I'll fry you. Survive, I'll fry you." She smiled and seemed satisfied. She handed the remote to one of the three males with the clipboards. Wrong move number one. "I created the variant. It was a total failure you know. Unfortunately, one of my former assistants leaked the variant out on the street. The idiot kept a blog. The one I produced gave the user enormous strength. The side effect was mindless aggression. The subject you encountered had some control over his faculties. With this new batch I scaled down the aggression, but kept the strength. Adding a Meth-variant and cannabis extracts may be the missing ingredients. You my annoying gumshoe will be the first test subject. . ."

I rocked the chair in an attempt to loosen the ropes.

Reanders put her face inches from mine. Her breath was that of coffee. "I hate you so much. Success or not you won't live to talk. Because you are a hothead I can easily fake your death in many ways and make it look like it was your idiotic self that did it. And , No. Your Vadnez did not call me." She let that sink in.

She stood up and flipped a few switches on

some machines and monitors to the side of me. She had the other two stooges attach wires to me. She walked over to the table and picked up the beaker of rage in one hand. A small sponge at the end on a long neck surgical scissor was in the other. "This new batch doesn't require injection or ingestion. It's topical."

I bucked the chair.

Reanders backed away. "Guy, hold this silly bitch still, please."

He reached out to grab me and I pivoted on the back left leg. I bucked up and landed the right front leg on his instep. His head came down and I flipped my head up. His arms flung out knocking Reanders' beaker of rage into her face. I pivoted several more times and was able to stand on my feet. I pushed off using my toes and had enough lift to rotate the chair forty-five degrees to the floor. I landed hard.

Reanders screamed in pain.

I removed the tied broken pieces from my arms and legs and ripped off all that wiring that had been attached to me. I spotted my purse and grabbed it. The Glock was still there.

Reanders was having a hard time though. She was curled up in a ball moaning. Her staff surrounded her. One reached down to touch her.

Her hand whipped out and caught him by the collar. "You didn't push the button." She growled.

He tried to escape.

"You didn't push the button!" She stood up and back handed him.

He went limped and crumpled to the ground.

She turned toward me. Her face twisted up in rage. "Now that was fuckin' dumb."

I replied, "Of you, it was. Whatcha expect, Psycho?"

Her eyes snapped wide open. I just pushed the wrong button.

She shoved the others out of her way and came at me like a freight train.

I dodged several wild swings but got hit on the fourth one. It hit my right arm. The hit was nothing like before. This one hurt.

She was wild and random with her swings. Most I could block, some I couldn't. I went on the attack and rained punches and kicks down on her. None effective enough to put her down. I decided the next best course of action was to run. I nearly reached the door when she grabbed me by the collar and jerked hard. I flown back into her watching and now surprised staff. I pulled my Glock out. I was in the process of aiming when it was snatched out of my hand. I scrambled for

I popped the spent clip out of the Glock and reloaded with a full clip. Too late, she sped past me headed up E 118 St.

I spotted a man next to a parked Smartcar. I ran over to him. "UN Agent Karen Bechard." I showed him my ID. "I need your car."

He said, "Yeah, right. You kiddin' me?"

Then I showed him my gun. "Get in the passenger side or get outta my way."

He slide over to the passenger side and handed me his keys. I gunned the engine and popped the gear into drive.

"If I total this one I'll have my Boss buy you a new car."

He snapped on his seat belt. "If I live through this I want a Tesla Model-S."

E 118th was a one-way street big enough for one car with parking on both sides. Traffic was light as Reanders crossed rapidly over Madison. The light was still green for me so I stumped on the accelerator and zipped past other cars. Reanders, however, muscled her way through traffic. She sideswiped several cars causing small pile ups. I took the sidewalk and easily maneuvered past all the chaos. I was catching up when she made a sudden left turn on Park Ave.

I overshot and decided to catch her by way of Lexington. I made the left turn and drove on the sidewalk. Lexington traffic was moving in the opposite direction.

"Holly Shit Lady. Who taught you how to drive?"

I just crossed 119st when I caught sight of the tail end of her car. School was still in session so I didn't have to worry about kids. I was just about to cross 120th when she flashed just in front of us. She was looking right at me as she slide across the intersection. She was trying to hit us.

I made a sharp right and followed. 3rd came up and she took the left fast.

"Watch out!" My passenger yelled.

I missed an old man on a walker. "Thanks. Hey, what's your name?"

He clenched the dashboard and looked terrified.

"Hey!" I said loudly. "I do this all the time. What is your name?"

"Andy! Andy, is my name! Holy . . . Lady!"

"Call me Karen." We swerved right then left.

Reanders was clipping cars and causing crashes in the process. I wondered where she was headed to. Then I heard the sirens. NYPD was near. We made it to the end of 3rd and made the right onto E 128th. She was making her way to 2nd ave when a M15 Bus pulled out of the depot. She tried to avoid the bus but it was too late. The Dodge hit the passenger front tire dead center. Airbags deployed inside.

I slid the Smart car to a stop and jumped out.

Reanders staggered out as I reached her.

She shook off her daze and started to rage.

I was prepared this time and kicked her squarely in the chest.

She lost her breath but swung at me. A near miss.

I came in close and kneed her in the crotch. I spun and kneed her in the temple. She dropped to her knees and I finished her off with an elbow to the head. A killing blow that should have ended the fight. She took the hit and dropped to the ground. Seconds later NYPD was upon us. I yelled out, "UN Agent Bechard."

Several more officers ran up to us guns drawn.

"My ID is in that Smartcar over there."

An officer bent down to check Reanders' pulse.

I said, "Be careful, she's high."

He pulled his hand back. Reanders grabbed it and pulled hard. He wrist broke. She grabbed his gun and was about to shoot when I knife chopped her in the throat. The gun dropped and several other cops rushed her. It took a total of ten to hold her down. Moments later it was over. Reanders was in the backseat of a squad car wearing six handcuffs. They had to place handcuffs on her ankles as well.

Andy walked up to me with my purse in hand. "Karen, that was some tough shit you put me through. Fuck, that was tight."

I took my purse, "Thanks. Some days are better than others." Just then my official cell rang. It was Vadnez.

"Karen speaking."

"Ms. Bechard, I see everything has ended well with minimal damage."

"Yay for the good guys. There is a certain car I used that will have to be repaired. Replacing it would be better."

There was a long pause, "Please fill out the necessary paperwork when you get back. I have some disturbing news and a new assignment."

"About this . . ."

Vadnez interrupted, "Only over secure lines. I'll expect you back in an hour. Your car is waiting in the employee parking lot."

"Thanks." I ended the call. I looked up to Andy. "Andy, thanks for the use of your car.

Here's my card. First chance you get, leave a message with name, address, insurance company name, policies, yada yada yada. The system will walk you through everything." I turned to an officer. "Is there someone available to take me to the UN Building? A ride would really be appreciated."

He said, "Sure Agent Bechard. You can ride with us. The lieutenant just released us."

Thirty minutes later I was sitting in Vadnez office with dirty and blood stained clothing. I knew that Vadnez was fighting his inner demons, but I enjoyed the thought of pushing his neat freak button.

"Ms. Bechard, you could have changed into clean clothing first."

"Boss, I'm a dutiful soldier. You asked me to be here as soon as possible. Well, this is as soon as possible."

He coughed once. He took a folder that was neatly stacked on top of several more. "Reanders' was contracted by the US government to create a performance enhancing drug that also increased endurance. It looks like she was very close. I should be getting a report from the CDC by week's end. I asked for a meeting with the CDC

Director and head of UNODC."

"And now that I made chaos sooner than later the America won't be getting their new drug."

"On the contrary. They've got it. And for free." He handed me the folder. "Your new assignment. Holders can finish up here."

The cover had a picture of Los Angeles. "When do I leave?"

"Tomorrow morning. Your ticket is inside the folder."

I opened it and sure enough. LA coach. I'll be upgrading thank you very much. I got up and started toward the door.

"Ms. Bechard?"

I stopped and turned. "Yes, sir?"

"The variant is worse than we thought. Los Angeles looks to be ground Zero. So far 35 cases in the last three days. Be very careful."

I nodded. "I'm always . . . "

" . . . rattling cages, yes." He finished.

He cares. I walked out the door. I was halfway down the hall when I placed a call to LA. Jim didn't pick up so I left a message on his voicemail. "Hey Love, I'll be back in town sometime tomorrow, so ask her to sleep elsewhere and hide her panties better this time." I hung up and laughed. I know Jim was seeing someone else. I couldn't blame him. I'm hardly in LA and I'm just as horny and flirtatious as he is. More so actually. So, who am I to get upset if he had another girl? Hell, if she's pretty I'd do her myself. In fact, Mary had been on my mind. I had planned on taking her panties and then some.

I was outside heading toward the employee parking area. Cortez was on my cell, "I hear you had fun."

"You know I always have fun."

He laughed, "For others your kind of fun is a death sentence."

"It's karma," I said. "Pure and simple. Kiss puppies and babies, help the elderly, wish the best for everyone."

"Like I said. A death sentence for others. Anyway, I just sent you Mary's home and cell number. She finished debriefing and the Airline gave her several weeks off. She's based out of LA."

"Really?"

"And get this. She has a ticket to LA tomorrow morning." He paused.

"You got me my ticket, didn't you?"

"Always got your back Girl. Always."

"Thanks, Cortez. See you when I get back.

Lunch, your choice."

"I see lobster in my future. One more thing."

"Yes?"

"Pack tactical."

"Really? That serious?"

"There's a lot of movement at all levels. The US may be mobilizing. It's the End of Day scenario."

"Shit."

"And then some."

After several rings Mary answered. "Hello?"

"Mary, this is Karen . . ."

She rushed out, "Karen! Oh my God! I was hoping you'd find a way to reach me. I tried getting your number, but I couldn't find anyone at the UN building who would even acknowledge UN Agents."

"Mary, Mary. You got me now."

"Oh Karen, I'm leaving for LA in the morning. I was afraid I'd never hear from you."

"What are you doing right now?"

"Just finished packing. I'm too worn out for TV."

"May I pick you up for that Dinner?"

"Of course, but I have an early flight."

"So do I."

"Huh?"

"We're on the same flight. What to do a sleepover?" Say yes, please.

She giggled. "I'd love to do a sleepover."

Sleepover was better than I had hoped for. Mary was a tigress and she made me her gazelle. Jim is a good kisser, but there is something about kissing another woman. It's the same, but different. The taste is different. So is the texture and smell. It's the total package that keeps me in the game, otherwise I'd stay on one side of the fence.

The gun is back

Mary and I made it just in time to board. We didn't have to go through the regular TSA lines. I had my way and she had her's. That shaved off about an hour. Last night I upgraded both our seats to World Class Business. Actually, I upgraded mine. Mary I had to buy a new ticket. But because she was an employee and there were two unsold WBC seats available the airline gave it to me at price. For once, Mary would be pampered. She almost didn't take the offer, but I persuaded her. I told her I have an unlimited budget - not quite the truth, and I could write this off as business related - a total lie. She gave in and the rest of the night was blissful. While on the flight Mary had a hard time just being a passenger. She wanted to help and I had to gently remind her she was a passenger. The other Flight Attendants would always shoo her back into her seat. One of them said, "Mary, yesterday you were a co-pilot. Today you are a passenger. Forever you are my hero. Now get back to your seat and relax." After two hours in the air she finally adjusted and just let it all be.

Other than a few bumps our flight was uneventful. I was able to finally absorb all the info in the folder Vadnez gave me. It was the Four Horsemen riding hard toward humanity. What do you do when you know a time bomb drug that randomly sparks apocalyptic armageddon zombie nightmares into reality is out there? Reanders' Bath Salt variant was scary. With regular Bath Salts it was rage and sex when something went wrong. With her street variant it was rage and random acts. Then a thought occurred to me. Reanders said Meth and Marijuana negated each other. It was caffeine that interested her. I made a phone call from the seat phone. Cortez answered switchboard. "Is Vadnez in his office?"

"Negatory. He stepped out a few hours ago. Need to pass on a message? He's in a meeting with the CDC and UNODC."

My heart raced. "Yeah, tell him Reanders was very interested in caffeine." Then a thought occurred. "Cortez, who was our rager?"

Cortez said, "Our John Q Public was a Mr. Phillip Michael Hunt."

"That's a real name?"

"You've heard the jokes too?" His laugh was almost like Guy's. He cleared his throat, "Anyway, Mr. Hunt was an average Joe. Troublesome youth, but nose clean through adulthood. He got caught up in the grunge scene and never left. He was on a trip to visit his girlfriend, CPL Kelly Stanford, stationed in Germany. She just finished rotation from Afghanistan. She hasn't received news yet.

"Oh."

"Yeah, total suckage."

"You have access to his credit card records?"

He said, "Karen, still a human of little faith. Yeah, he bought coffee at the Airport Starbuck's. Grande. He used his Starbuck's card. He drinks it by the gallon."

"Thanks, Cortez."

"Two more thing."

"Yes?"

"Reanders' escaped shortly after you captured her. The two officers are okay, but hospitalized. The paper trail shows that she may be in Vegas, LA, or DC. We're not sure yet. She has a dozen private jets and they all left within minutes of one another."

"Who's on it?"

"Vadnez left it to the FBI, lest we tread on US sovereignty."

"And the second thing?"

"Reanders lied about the former assistant. I checked. Dr. Piper is still on the payroll. She has an office in Century City. She also has a fully functional research lab in Santa Monica. One and one is adding up to oh shit."

"I agree. Cortez, always got good Intel."

"Only for my best girl. When you get to LA don't do anything I wouldn't do, and if you do, don't get caught."

"Never."

"Ha!" He ended the call.

A lot to think about. Reanders on the loose. I fear no man, but this woman was different. What do you get when you mix scary-genius with rage? The End of Days? December 21st was around the corner. I needed to think about something else. I looked over to Mary. She had headphones on and was getting into the 'I'm just a regular passenger' role. That made me feel better and I tried to think about all things good. Scary-genius kept coming up so I stopped trying to fight it. And I thought of different ways to end her life. Bullet to the head, to the heart, throat cut, decapitation, strangulation? All made me feel better and I was finally able to relax until we landed.

Jim was waiting for us at baggage. I told Mary about Jim and I warned Jim about Mary. Both were good with it so that made life easy. He waved and I ran to him. He caught me and I tried to slip my tongue down his throat. He returned the kiss likewise.

Mary reached us and said, "We need to get a room if you keep this up. And I so want some more."

Jim broke first and gave Mary his best grin. "Mary, so nice to meet you."

"He means it. That's not a real gun in his pocket."

Mary looked down. "OMG Karen, eight inches is really eight inches."

Jim blushed. "Ladies, please."

Mary and I laughed. Then a horrible thought occurred. Suppose Mary and Jim hit it off. She's based in LA and she'll be able to see him more often. Oh, man Karen. What have you done?

I was pretty quiet during the car ride. Both noticed.

Mary asked, "Karen, what's up?"

I smiled, "Nothing. Just enjoying the moment." While I had a tight and muscular body, Mary's was smooth. She was toned but with just enough fat to make her hot. She had a nice butt and I loved her breasts. They were perfect on her.

Mary leaned in closer. "You sure?"

I leaned in too. "Of course." and I kissed her on the nose. Now I hadn't even considered Jim's feelings on this. Here I am coming "home" and bringing toys. Most men would love to be in Jim's shoes right about now and I'm doubly sure later tonight. But how did Jim feel about this. "Jim," I said.

"Yeah."

"I am being pretty selfish. How are you with all this?"

Mary sat quietly.

He looked over at both of us. "Karen. At first I wasn't sure what to think. But this is you. And I'm okay with that."

I stared back.

"Seriously. I'm okay. I've learned that anyone you want me to include in our circle will be included. Period. And you do give me lots of space which I really do appreciate." After a few seconds he added, "Friday and Number of the Beast."

Now I felt better, both of my favorite Heinlein books. I wasn't sure if Mary got the reference.

She laughed, "Too weird."

I said, "Huh?"

She answered, "Time enough for Love and Stranger in a Strange Land, my two favorites."

Jim and I laughed. I did make a good move.

We got to Jim's apartment before Noon. Luckily, Jim had the day off. Timing is everything. He parked in front of his new F150 and we carried all our luggage up three flight of stairs. I had a large suitcase with clothes and accessories and medium suitcase with work-related gear. I used a tactical messenger bag as a purse on this trip. Mary had her large luggage and a small tote bag. Once inside the apartment we deposited them on the living room floor. Jim walked into the kitchen when his phone rang.

"Damn! I hope this is Mom." He answered, "Yes?" Seconds ticked by. "Seriously?" More seconds. "Give me thirty . . . no thirty. Not sooner. Sorry, no I can't just drop this one. . . And if I didn't answer the phone? . . . yeah . . . exactly! . . . no less than thirty. . . is it required . . . Sarge, push me and . . . thank you! See you soon." He hung up and looked grim.

I looked at him, "It's started?"

"That's why you are here isn't it?"

I nodded.

He walked over to me and kissed me like never before. Then he turned to Mary. She leaned in and he kissed her with just as much passion. Then he stood straight and got ready for work.

Mary said, "What just happened?"

"Our nightmare, serious shit."

"Nightmare?" She said.

I nodded, "Have a seat."

She did.

"You know I work for the UN."

She nodded.

"You've seen me in action."

She nodded again. "I'm sure it was only the tip of the iceberg."

"The guy on the airplane is a small part of this."

Her eyes grew big.

"You've heard of bath salts?"

"He was on that?"

I nodded.

"My brother-in-law tried that before Oregon made it illegal and he never, I mean never, acted like that."

"Really?"

"My sister said he'd hit on the weekends. She tried it a few times and said she hallucinated colors for hours. She didn't like the afterglow and gave it up."

"You've tried it?"

"Nah, we drug test regularly. Even night binge-drinking is discouraged. I don't even smoke pot."

"Mr. Hunt . . . "

"That was passenger Hunt? OMG, sorry, continue."

I smiled, "I'd never name my kid with that combination."

She nodded.

"Well, Mr. Hunt was on a variant of the drug. He had other chemicals in his system which may have triggered his rage."

"Wow," was what I got.

"Your sister and brother-in-law coffee drinkers?"

"He isn't, but my sister is."

I thought about that. "History of Meth?"

"Thank God, no! Nasty stuff. They both do marijuana when the kids are not around or asleep."

Jim came out of the bathroom. He had packed

a duffle bag, probably clothes and things, and dropped it by the door. He was wearing sweats. I figured he'd change at the station. "I have twenty minutes before I go." He smiled.

I licked my lips and said, "Plenty for me. Don't know about Mary."

She picked up on the cue, "I'm there in ten."

Jim stepped up to us and kissed me first, then Mary.

"Mary," I said. "The gun is back."

She giggled and pulled his sweat pants and underwear down. Jim nearly poked us in the eyes.

"And fully loaded."

We both giggled and did our thing. Jim did his job and satisfied us in fifteen. We finished him minutes later.

There are people eating people out there

After Jim left, Mary and I continued. We took our time and just enjoyed the moment. Around 3:00 pm my official cell went off. It was Cortez.

"Karen, channel 9 news, quick."

I fumbled for the remote and tuned Jim's 60" flat screen to channel 9.

" . . . again, LAPD has quarantined skidrow. All traffic has been halted into and out of anywhere east and south of Main and 3rd and west and north of Alameda and 7th street. CDC has been called in. There are reports of vicious attacks and acts of cannibalism coming in. LA County Sheriff, LAPD, LA Fire department and other organizations have mobile units in front of City Hall. There's talk about bringing in the National Guard . . .."

I turned the TV off.

I told Cortez, "I'm on it."

He said, "Be safe. Out."

Mary was looking at me wide eyed. She was scared. "Is this real?"

I nodded. "I gotta go."

She grabbed me, "Please no Karen. This shit scares me."

"Mary, look, this is what I do. I put myself in harm's way. I have to assess the situation first hand."

She stared at me for a long time. She had the same look she did on the airplane. Then she wiped her eyes and said, "I'm coming with you."

"The hell you are!"

"Karen, I will not stay here by myself, and I gotta know. You seem to be one of the few people who are in the know. I flew shotgun with you for God Sake."

"Mary, please think this through. Most likely all the action is in Skidrow and not here."

"I don't care. I wan . . . no, need to be near you. I can help too."

I stared at her.

She stared back. "Karen, please."

I pointed out the window. "There are people eating people out there."

"I ate you didn't I?!?"

Well, that knocked the wind out of my sails. I softened my tone, "Ummm, that's different."

"Eating is eating." And she dared me to answer back.

Instead I kissed her. "Have you ever fired a pistol?"

"My sister taught me. Nine, ten, forty-five, three-fifty-seven, shotgun, M16-A2, a handful of rifles."

Okay I was convinced. "Seriously, this is worse than real. You saw how the guy was on the plane."

She answered, "Headshot, end of rage."

I nodded and got my medium bag. The large one had my clothes. This one was work related. I plopped it on the bed. I had a special lock on the bag. It had the UN seal and my agent number. I unlocked it. Mary's eyes went wide when I opened it.

"They let you travel with that type of arsenal?"

"Yeah, neat, huh?"

She reached in and pulled out my M4A1. "I'll take this one."

I laughed. "Not this?" I pulled out a Kahr Limited Edition Pink Pistol.

"And that too! It's so cute. That's my backup gun."

I pulled out two Glock 20s. "Mine." Next came my 15 inch hunting knife plus my Ka-Bar. I took out my short sword, some stars, a few throwing blades, duty belt, boots, gloves, bodysuit. The tactical vest came out last with a light level 3-A kevlar vest. "Sorry, I only brought one vest."

"Then can I have one of those nasty looking knives?"

I had an extra 15-inch Jungle Master. I gave it to her along with a small walkie-talkie. I pocketed two and placed my short-nosed Smith & Wesson .357 in a back holster. It was a seven-shooter and my backup.

Five minutes I was set to dish out death. Mary had black tights and a black tank. With her black biker books and my Jungle Master strapped to her leg she looked tough. Me, I was downright scary. Something out of a GI Joe comic book.

"Ready?"

"Ready."

We took Jim's F150.

Thirty minutes later we pulled up to a road

block. I presented my ID. It took several minutes to verify my credentials. I found a spot and backed the truck into it. Mary and I got out and walked to one of the command post. Everybody was represented, including the FBI. "Who's in charge?" I asked. I figured the Mayor and Chief of Police would be in RACR feeding pertinent data to this mobile post.

A few hands pointed to a Mobile Command Unit that had LAPD markings. We walked over. I showed my ID. Donaldson turned around.

"Well, Karen! Not surprised to see you. Nice flying, but your landing sucked. Jim told me you might make your way down here."

"I'm here talking to you. Doesn't that mean anything? What's the news?"

"Scary, that's what. We got a dozen teams going in pulling people out. There's groups of Ragers, that's what we are calling them, roaming the streets."

"Groups?"

"Yeah, don't know how many. RACR spotted about twenty. Small arms is only effective in headshots."

"You in charge?"

"The Commander is. He's in the Van. Let me introduce you."

We followed Donaldson up a small set of stairs. The MCU was abuzz with activity. One side had a bank of cubicles with chairs and monitors. One individual was talking into a walkie-talkie.

"Unit two, proceed. RACR gave clearance. Nothing in sight for at least a block."

Donaldson cleared his throat.

The Commander was seasoned with weathered skin, but his eyes were crystal sharp. He gave me one look, "Bechard, right?"

Quick. "I am and you, sir?"

He kept his eyes on one of the monitors. "Unit Five hold that position. RACR hasn't cleared it yet."

He looked over to me. "Richardson. You here to take over, get in the way, or help."

"Get in the way. UN Observer, but I'll do Tactical and or Rescue."

He looked over to Mary. "Civilian?"

"Assistant. Name is Hernandez. She can be a runner as well as provide shooter backup."

He gave me one more look, "Approved. Donaldson, they're yours."

We followed Donaldson. Before we reached the door Richardson started shouting. "Unit Five, fall back. Herd coming your way from 5th and

Wall St. North. Fall back west."

I stopped and turned. I could see the herd Richardson was talking about on the monitor. They were running toward a group of about six officers. Richardson said, "What the devil." There's another herd. They'll be closed in. "Unit Five. Go immediately east. New herd closing in from west. Run! Run!"

We watched in horror and disbelief as the six officers ran. The monitor switched to a different camera angle.

Oh shit I thought. They're not going to make it.

Within a minute everyone was in eyesight of one another. Unit Five started shooting.

I heard over the walkie-talkie, "Unit Two on the way to assist. Over."

Richardson spoke out loud, but in a low volume. "Not sure if they're going to make it." He turned to Donaldson, "We have any spare units to assist."

"No, Sir. All the units are out."

"I need a mobile to assist."

I spoke up. "We can do that. I have Jim's Truck keys in my hand. What's the radio frequency?"

Richardson gave it to me.

Mary and I ran to Jim's Truck.

"Ready Girl?"

"Ready."

I pulled out and headed to an inner barricade. Richardson radioed ahead for them to move the barrier. We sped past the cement blocks. I had the walkie talkie in my shirt pocket with a white earpiece stuck in my ear. Mary had her's on the opposite side. I heard Richardson of the radio.

He named us Mobile Two, interesting. I briefly wondered what happened to the first Mobile Two.

I turned down Wall St and saw about twenty of them. Blood covered and torn clothes. Blood on their faces and hands. The movies got the image better, but real life was scarier. I gunned the engine and rammed them. They were doomed souls anyway. I just sped them closer to that end. I took out about half with one being tossed into the bed of the truck. He got up, raging, smashed a hand through the back window. Must have broken every bone in that hand. He grabbed my collar and pulled. Mary stuck her gun through the opening and blurped a set of rounds through his skull. The hand slacked and let go. I saw several more and ran them down too. Then I saw the officers. Four were dragging two while shooting Ragers. I stumped on the accelerator and took out three more. Mary and I finished the rest off with head shots.

"Get in and someone toss the deadweight out in the back."

They put the two wounded in the back. Two sat up with us in the cabin. I stumped the accelerator again and sped up Wall St. Two Ragers had the nerve to try and compete with metal. Both lost.

I told the two Officers in the back, "I'm UN Agent Bechard. This is Ms. Hernandez, my partner."

"I'm Officer McKinley, this is Rogers. Cass, Dean, Jones, Sanchez, are in the back. Thanks, we owe you."

We had three blocks to go. "Do you know an Officer Jim Anderson?"

"This is some mad shit out here. Yeah, I do. He's with Unit Twelve. They took a Hummer further in. We got thousands of people out there. Most were able to lock themselves into various buildings. Office buildings and hotels are secure. We have dozens of units safeguarding those. But there are some with limited shelter. Some liquor and grocery store owners were able to lock some patrons and themselves in freezers and meat lockers, but of course we're gonna have to get them out eventually. It's the smaller shops and motels that got hit hard. Some folks are locked in cars and vans. They're safe only because they hadn't been discovered yet by these Ragers. Those are the ones we're trying to get to and extract."

We made it to the barriers. I stopped outside a medical unit.

Mary asked, "Why so many?"

McKinley answered, "So many? There are hundreds of them running rampage. I'd call them Zombies but they run!"

"Haven't they tried to get out?"

"Yeah. And we stop them each time with deadly force. It's like the mind is still working but amped on anger juice. They attack then suddenly they all know when to stop. Eerie."

We got out and walked over to the Command Unit. Richardson was waiting. Some spots RACR couldn't see.

McKinley said, "Commander, all dead. The camper was ripped to shreds. Body parts everywhere."

Someone from the Command Unit yelled out. "We got another 911. Not too far from here."

Donaldson said, "Mobile two is the only one

on this side of the barrier."

Then we heard over the radio, "Mobile eleven coming in with survivors . . . this is Mobile Twenty . . . eta two minutes. Gonna need EMTs . . ." I pulled the earpiece away and draped it over my shoulder.

"Directions?"

"On the roof of the Weldon Hotel, Maple and E 5th Ave. Take Wall and make a right on 5th."

Mary and I ran to the truck. McKinley and Rogers were already in the back seat. This time they were dressed in Riot Gear, had M16s, two pistols, and some flash bang grenades.

I started the truck and popped it in Drive. We zipped past the barriers and headed toward Wall St.

I put the earpiece back in. " . . . Unit Thirty secure for the moment. We have eight-four civilians. Three are hurt, but not critical. Mobile Two you got company. Five News copters are following you."

Great I thought. Just what I needed.

I took 5th pretty sharply then slide onto Maple. I slammed the brakes and stopped just in front of the entrance. McKinley and Rogers got out and took position just inside the building.

McKinley said, "Get them we'll hold."

As Mary and I walked through the carnage I made sure we both had an earplug in our free ear. We stepped through some really nasty stuff - blood and guts everywhere. We found the stairs. In the distance we could hear them raging. I couldn't tell how many but I knew it was one too many. With Glocks in hand I started up the stairs. Mary had my back with the M4 at the ready. It was like she was born to do this. Her sister was a great teacher.

After a few minutes we made it to the top and about five were pounding on the roof fire door. I aimed and made three immediate headshots. Two turned and jumped down the flight of stairs raging. One caught the pistol in his mouth. Trigger squeezed and that ended him. The last one had his arms raised. Mary blurped the M4 and half his head was gone.

We made it to the door. I yelled , "The stairwell is clear. We need to get you out now."

The door didn't open.

I yelled, "UN Agent Bechard with a rescue team. We need to leave now."

The door opened. I saw a collection of old and young men and women - all had lived a hard life.

"Follow me." I said and started down the

stairs. About half way down a door opened. It was a Rager. Mary took him out with one shoot. The girl was getting used to the M4A1's five pound trigger. We made it to the bottom floor. McKinley and Rogers just finished off about ten Ragers. It was maddening to think about why so many and why they are group thinking. It was beyond scary. We rushed outside. I did a quick head count. Thirteen plus us. The Truck was too small. "Okay," I said, "Mary you drive, McKinley, Rogers, and Myself will stay. Everyone else into the truck. Four up front, the rest in the back. Someone started to protest. I barked out, "Shut the fuck up and get in the back. Another word and I'll take you out."

No protest.

With the truck packed Mary took off.

McKinley, Rogers and I decided this was our home base. We pretty much had the building to ourselves and if necessary we had the roof as Plan B.

Off in the distance I saw a Honda accord driving up the street. All but one tire was blown, but it didn't matter. Something was lodged in the passenger wheel well. The wheel just spun casting smoke in the air. He was going nowhere fast. Idiot I thought. Reverse, then drive. The driver was probably in a panic and just wanted to get out. Then I spotted six Ragers rush the car. They started pounding on the hood and roof.

'Karen," I told myself, "Save lives." I told McKinley and Rogers to guard the building. "I'll be back," I said as I ran toward the car. The Ragers had managed to lift the car over their heads and toss the thing about ten feet. It landed on its side and the passenger window buckled then burst. One got on top of the car and ripped the door off.

Run Karen! Run!

He reached in and grabbed a man.

Karen, run! Faster! I stretched out my legs. Run, Karen, run!

He was about to bite the man in the neck.

I reached him in time. Bam! My Glock barked. Headshot. The man dropped back into the car.

I jumped on top of the car. Bam! Bam! Bam! Bam! Bam! All headshots. All Ragers dead. I helped the man, a woman, and three kids out - one boy and two girls, all scared. The little boy was holding a backpack. The top was partially opened. A small white mutt terrier poked its head out of the opening. I said, "We have to get to that building."

The man nodded, "Thank you! We thought we . . ."

I cut him off, "Welcome. Building. Focus."

He took a deep breath.

I was about to say ready when I spotted a dozen coming at us. If this was the time to say 'Oh, Shit.' I missed it. I grabbed the backpack and put it on. "Grab the kids." I said. The father picked up his son and one daughter. The Mom picked up the other daughter. I said, "No matter what happens you run for that building where the two officers are. This is serious. Don't stop period because your life depends on making it to that building." Both nodded. The group was now between us and the Hotel. I yelled, "Run!" I hadn't reloaded so the Guns were limited. I pulled out my short sword and hunting knife. Both had blade edge facing outward. I ran and hoped the family could keep up. To their credit the Mom and Dad did. Fear of death does that I guess. I put myself in the middle zone and made sure my mind was clear. We had another ten yards to go when I remembered a verse an instructor used a lot. The mean old bastard turned out to be very poetic at times. 'I am leaving you with a gift— peace of mind and heart. And the peace I give is a gift the world cannot give. So don't be troubled or afraid.' and I thought of nothing. I reached the first two and slashed my blades. Head drop, head drop. I cut right - head drop, head drop. I moved to the left - heart pierced, arms gone, head drop. Then centerline - throat cut, arms gone. More came at me. Throat cut, head drop, heart pierced. I lost count, but I kept centered and let instinct and muscle memory guide me. Head drop, head drop. I was Lady Death today and gave a lot of it. Hands grabbed at the Father and I sliced up. Arms gone, head drop. Another tried for the Mother. I sliced down and cut through the entire torso. I cut sideways and just worked the blades. The Mom and Dad ran faster. The kids screamed. I heard the Father yell, "No!" And he bit down hard on a hand that had grabbed his daughter's shirt. I sliced up and the handgrip slacked. The father spat the hand out. I sliced again. Head drop, heart pierced, arms gone, throat cut, throat cut, head drop, throat cut, arms gone, then nothing. All the kids were crying and terrified. We had another 30 yards to go to reach the building when a few more came at us. I heard a gunshot. Then two, then three. Ragers dropped at each gunshot. McKinley and Rogers were hitting dead center and dropping them. Several tried to sideswipe us. Three shots, three dead. Seconds later we made it to the building. I spoke into the walkie-talkie, "Mary, how's that ride?"

"Just dropped off my payload. Got more troops and heading your way."

Rogers looked over to me and said straight faced, "Agent Bechard, I want to have your baby." His mic was live.

I heard Jim's voice. "Sorry, but I'm having that baby." Just then Mary skidded to a stop. Jim jumped out and I ran to him still covered in blood.

He caught me and planted a wet kiss on my lips. "I expected you to be an observer, not part of the action."

I shrugged, "I'm not good at observing."

Mary had brought a SWAT team.

The Mother had lost a shoe during the run. She took off the other shoe and flung it toward the pile of dead Ragers. She cursed them all to hell, collected her kids and got into the truck.

Mary said, "After I drop the family off I have to deliver more troops to the front line. There's about a hundred of them gathering near 6th and Los Angeles St. LAPD and the LA County Sheriff located a new command center near there. It's on 6th and San Pedro." She hugged me and got back in the truck. "Be safe, Girl." And she was off.

I looked to Jim, "What's the plan?"

He said, "Captain Banner is in charge," and leaned his head toward an officer in full SWAT gear. He was talking to McKinley and Rogers. I walked up to him.

"Captain, UN Agent Bechard. I'm here to offer my assistance."

The Captain looked me up and down. "I think we got this one, Ms. Bechard. I'll request a runner to pick you up."

I was about to say something when McKinley spoke up. "Captain, no, we don't got this one. I'll fight with Agent Bechard anytime."

Rogers nodded.

The Captain looked perplexed. In ten seconds he marked himself as a sexist pig. I'd have to convince myself to save his ass when the fire got hot. McKinley pointed to the pile of bodies off in the distance. Banner looked. Then looked at me. He was in turmoil. "Military?"

"Army, the first Iraq War. Apache pilot. Trained with the South Korean 707 White Tiger Commandos. Trust me, I won't be the one in the way."

Jim said, "Wait. Karen. You?"

Rogers said, "It was fucking awesome. She ran through a dozen of those things. With fucking long blades and with a family running behind her!

And they came out alive! No cop here could have done that. If I had my choice I'd fight alongside Agent Bechard anytime. Anytime."

Banner huffed. I could have decked him, but he saved himself. "You wanna do point?"

"Wedge? What's the mission?"

"Yes or no?"

"I gave you my answer. Now tell me the objective."

He looked at Jim and said, "Feisty one. Bet she's a tigress."

Jim didn't answer. I saw he had his own turmoil to work through.

Banner coughed. "We're going to start clearing out buildings and looking for survivors. Once we clear a building we'll get a runner to move out survivors, if any."

While he was talking I filled my magazines to capacity.

"G.I Jane here will take point. You officers will take rear. We'll do a wedge formation through the streets. Once inside a building the Officers will guard our Xville. The Agent here will work point. We'll clear rooms in alternate. Any questions?"

"Are we ready yet?" I asked.

"Just for that you can kick your own doors

in."

I smiled and walked into the Hotel.

"Wait," He said. "This building hasn't been cleared?"

"Nope. We went in and rescued thirteen civilians. Encountered some Ragers. Might be more and since we are here this might as well be the first building."

He grunted his approval

I pulled out my right holstered Glock and switched on the flashlight and laser pointer. Jim and the other Officers guarded our rear. Banner and the rest of the SWAT team followed me. I checked behind the counter and saw body parts and dried blood. I walked through the first floor. The first door was locked. Banner's smirk disappeared when I kicked the door off its hinges. Messy bed, unflushed toilet, half packed luggage. I heard the next room door kicked in. It took two tries. This one was clear and I yelled out "Clear!" I heard several more clears and was once more point going up the stairs to the second floor. We repeated this all the way through to the roof. The Hotel had two elevators and we split off to ride them down to the bottom. Banner radioed in and said the Hotel was clear and for a runner to send in a guard group to hold the position. We would make this our home base. A few minutes later Mary showed up with a dozen National Guard soldiers. Banner wanted them to guard the hotel until we returned. And that was exactly how we would do this. Check, clear, bring in the Guards to maintain. Mary was busy and that was good. She was one of a dozen runners that kept a steady stream of soldiers, cops, and survivors moving throughout the entire area.

It was the sixth building we went into that turned bad. I heard the scream first and rushed forward. The building was a local drug store and several Ragers had broken through the back door. One was about to bite down on a woman's neck when I hit him in the head with the butt of my gun. He lifted up his head and I made him eat the barrel. The Glock barked once and he hit the floor like a sack of potatoes. One thing I found interesting was that there were no women Ragers. Not one. The woman I saved was hysterical. She latched onto me and nearly choked me. I heard several other shoots in the distance.

"It's okay, it's okay."

She sobbed harder into my shoulder.

"Is there anyone else alive?"

She cried harder. I lifted her chin up and gave

her a sharp short slap to the face. She stopped crying.

"Is there anyone else around?" I asked.

She blinked a few times. "Maybe. We ran in here and waited for hours. Then one of the women went crazy and rushed out the door. A few minutes later those things rushed in. Then you came in."

A few minutes later we cleared this building. Banner called in a runner for guards and retrieval. It was getting dark now and that just turned scary up a notch.

He looked out to the street. I knew what he was thinking. I walked up next to him.

"Forward or base camp?"

"Our odds just got worse if we continue. . . " I knew he was scared. Who wouldn't be. Raging maniacal cannibals in the dark? Then we heard over the radio. "All units return to your home bases. Runners will bring food, ammo, and sleep gear. Report your location by the numbers." We were group twenty. Banner had sent the group of Guardsmen to the last cleared building. He wanted to be sure it stayed cleared. Thirty minutes later Mary showed up. She made us her last run. She jumped out and gave me a big hug. "I'm staying the night here."

I smiled. Best way to end the day.

Banner walked up to us. He had been talking to Jim and the others for some time. "You and Anderson can have first watch street level. Ms. Hernandez here is free to leave."

Mary said, "I'll stay thank you. I'll do first watch with Karen."

He stared at her for a few seconds, smiled, and said, "Very well. McKinley and Rogers will relieve you in four hours."

The old prev had probably undressed Mary and bedded her within those seconds.

He walked off.

I looked at my watch. It was eight and the sunlight was fading too fast.

We used lobby chairs and couches as barriers. I was stationed on the right side, Jim left. Mary was our runner and kept us both engaged. We were close enough to talk in normal voice.

Once we settled in Jim said, "Karen, I'm sorry."

I would have guessed he was talking about me being Lady Death.

"Sorry about my reaction this afternoon."

I said, "Jim, you didn't know. Remember I don't talk about my work or what I do."

He replied, "Not that. When Banner made that

sexist remark."

That got me for a loop. "Jim, no need, it was none of his business."

"I should have said something."

"I'm glad you didn't. Jim, seriously, I'm glad you didn't. It worked out better that you didn't say a thing. Besides, we're on watch together. He figured it out and has a soft spot in the middle of that iron heart of his."

He was silent for a moment. "You know, this is the first time we've worked together."

I liked that about Jim. He was sentimental and very romantic. True, we really didn't know much about it each. I'd fly in for a few days or we were able to take some time off together, but we never really engaged one another on the personal stuff. We had a lot in common and that made it easier. It was the fine tuning we never had a chance to do, but so far I liked. He did his job well - he was a Police Officer Level 3, so someone in the department thought he was worth promoting. He was a wonderful lover and even let me bring Mary into our intimate circle. He was confident about himself. The fact that he apologized for not speaking up spoke volumes.

Mary came up and plopped herself on a chair between us. She was exhausted I knew.

I said while still looking out in the increasingly darkening street way. "How goes it?"

She replied, "It goes. You guys need anything? Food, water?"

"Not yet, a bath would help."

"That, girlfriend, we get at Midnight."

Luckily, we still had power. All the streetlights came on. A few minutes later, Banner came out.

"Word from RACR. The mass of Ragers that was assembling earlier has been dispersed. We killed over half and wounded most of the others. The CDC is on the scene and took surviving Ragers. What a blood spill. Tomorrow we clear more buildings but it looks like we may have gotten this thing under control."

I nodded.

He looked my way. "Bechard?"

"Yeah," I said without looking.

"I'm an old Soldier. It's hard for me sometimes to see women in harm's way."

"Something change your mind?"

He softly chuckled, "Check out the news when you're off shift." He left.

Mary said, "Something I missed?"

"Not really. Banner and I had a disagreement earlier."

She said, "Karen, you know you already got a

nickname."

"Really? What's the name?"

"G.I. Jane."

"Banner called me that earlier."

Jim spoke, "The Demi Moore movie?"

Mary said, "Yeah. It was a good movie. Pretty intense at some parts, but she did a good job."

"I really should be called UN Jane, if that's the case."

Jim took his eye off the street for a moment and looked at me. Then he looked back. I wondered if I scared him. Was he even into death wielding butches? He was deep into thought. Most times I dig what I can do. I can best most men in almost anything physical. I love wiping smirks and smiles off their faces when they say, 'Aw, look. A little woman." After I kick their asses they change their tune, "Aw, fuck. It's that bitch again." Which is totally fine by me, but I was having trouble with the thought of Jim rejecting me for the reasons I like being me.

We remained quiet for the remainder of our shift. McKinley, Rogers and one of the SWAT team members took over.

Rogers tapped me on the shoulder. "I was serious when I said I'd have your baby. If Anderson has issues, I don't."

I smiled and gave him a peck on the cheek. He turned deep red.

When I made it to the room designated as ours Mary was already in the shower. Her flashlight was aimed at the ceiling and that gave the bathroom enough light to see. Jim was sitting on the bed. He was still in his clothes. The TV was on and he was looking at a local news channel. I had forgotten about the News copters, but there I was. The whole scene of me saving the family. The Newscaster warned everyone the broadcast was graphic and disturbing. I thought, "Ya think?" There was a close up of my face and the Newscaster remarked how calm I was during the run. He, too, called me G.I. Jane. There was banter on who I could have been. One of them mentioned I was part of a covert department of the United Nations. I was certain Vadnez was having a cow. It didn't take much for me to imagine the lecture I'd get later. 'Ms. Bechard, we are observers, not participants.'

After watching the segment Jim looked over to me.

I was speechless.

He took off his clothes, laid them neatly on the back of a chair, and walked into the bathroom without saying anything. No expression at all.

Mary was still there hogging all the hot water.

I didn't know what to do. A few seconds later Jim called out. "Karen, why aren't you in here with us. Mary is using all the hot water."

I was so relieved. I took off my clothes and got a much needed wash down.

Buzzzzzzzzz, wrong answer

I didn't sleep all that well. Reanders had been
on my mind. Now that I had time to think it made
sense to assume Reanders was behind this. The
Ragers acted more like her than like someone
on Bath Salts. So that told me she was the one
dealing. What bothered me was the timing. She
escaped earlier, but that was not enough time
for her to land, set up shop, make the drug, and
distribute. She had to have been planning this
for a while, but needed more info, which I had. I
gave her the last piece of the puzzle she needed
to refine the drug. And those things are the result.
But that was the troubling part. Those things
had once been normal people. Some troubled
souls, some not, but still people. They were not
of their mind as Ragers. I, as Lady Death, ended
their torment and pain, but it still didn't sit well.
Reanders the Mad scientist. Murderer, dealer.
I so wanted to shoot her in the head, but that

would solve nothing. Not really. She needed to be captured alive.

It was four in the morning when I decided to get up. I got dressed and decided to go downstairs. Banner and two other SWAT Team members just relieved McKinley, Rogers, and the other team member.

Banner looked over his shoulder. "Couldn't sleep, Princess?"

I gave him a smile. "Nope. I'll have some unfinished business to take care of after this."

"You know, I find it interesting that the United Nations would have a representative here, at this time."

"Not so strange," I said. "Believe it or not, I'm often in LA and not just for vacation. Los Angeles is a cosmopolitan of sorts. It should be considered one of the World's capitals."

"That so? You know something about these things?"

"Who happen to be people gone bad."

"That, too."

"I do. That's why I'm here."

"Can you tell me anything?"

I thought for a few seconds. "It's a drug. A variant of Bath Salts . . ."

"That I figured. But the number of these things

and the way they work together sometimes . . ."

"Is the result of a tailored drug probably destined to the US Military. At least it was before all this."

"No shit?"

"Yes shit. And I need to find the creator."

He thought for some time. Then he said, "Bechard. You're alright by me. The city keeps me as a mushroom. You know, I'm kept in the dark and fed bullshit. I'm told to perform. Most times I never see the big picture. Like today. I just knew we had to shoot monsters and rescue people. Nothing about the whys this started to begin with. But you. You got the big picture and your sights on the cause. I saw that news feed of you today. That was some nice work."

"Thanks."

"I would never have had to balls to run head long into that crowd. Forgive me for my behavior earlier."

"Done."

He paused for a moment and sighed. "My daughter would be about your age . . ."

"You're that old?"

"Yeah. Retirement is around the corner. But she's serving in Afghan. And everyday I pray she misses some IED. We talk once a week, but man it's hard. After seeing you perform today, I know, with the right training, woman can do just as well as men. But it's still a hard pill to swallow."

I gave him a light punch to the shoulder. "Coffee?"

"Yeah, please. Black."

I walked back into the lobby. Earlier Mary had cleaned as much as she could. The Pot had about two cups left. I pour Banner and myself a cup and made more coffee for the others. The flies hadn't discovered us yet, but I was sure today would be the day. Flies and the smell. Disgusting combo.

I walked out and handed Banner his cup. "Another pot is brewing."

He nodded and sipped his cup.

I did likewise.

Then we heard a shot off in the distance.

Followed by several more.

Then automatic fire. The radio crackled, "Hold your position."

The shoots were about a block away, about another five buildings after the last one we checked.

Then we heard the screams.

I raced upstairs to get Mary and Jim, both were already dressed and headed my way.

"Morning. It begins." And they followed me

downstairs.

The radio crackled again, "Hold that line. Hold that . . ." Static and the automatic fire stopped.

Then we heard, "All Law Enforcement units pull back to home base. Pull back. Military personnel will hold ground. Ground forces are on the way."

McKinley and Rogers were already in the truck. Jim was going to take driver when I said I think I should. He only thought about it for a second then handed me the keys. Mary sat between us and the SWAT team sat in the rear box.

Banner yelled, "I hope you can drive like you can fight."

I revved the engine, yelled back, "Better!" and dropped the gear into D4.

A dozen Ragers stood in front of us. Not one moved. I turned sharply left and caught the glimpse of something heavy behind them. Now they're thinking Ragers? That was a sobering thought. Banner called through the radio, "Why didn't you ram those bastards?"

"It was a trap. They were sacrificing themselves."

We had another two blocks to go when I spotted another dozen just standing there.

I spoke in the walkie-talkie, "I don't like this." One block left, then I saw the Helicopters, Homeland Security and Military. Marine Hummers drove past us along with several tanks. A dozen five tons, and deuce and a halves rumbled by. We made it to the barrier and home base had been transformed into a Military outpost. The troops arrived, for better or worse. I pulled up next to the LAPD Command Unit.

Richardson walked out. He looked like he hadn't slept in days. "The Military is running this rodeo now. We're to stand down and do clean up later. Their gonna clear the area out in mass."

Just then my cell phone went off. It was Cortez. I said, "Excuse me, this might be important." I walked a few feet away, "Karen speaking."

Cortez said, "I think they should call you UN Jane. More accurate."

"Really? I was thinking that last night."

He laughed, "You know, Vadnez is beside himself. He said the F word."

"Seriously?"

"Yeah, but not for obvious reasons. Credit was given to the LAPD for saving that family. And that a UN Operative may have stepped over the political line. The SG called Vadnez to his office an hour ago. Both want to see you as soon as you wrap up your case there."

Interesting that I was to report after I wrapped up my case.

"By your silence you find it interesting that Vadnez said after you wrap up your case. Through me for a loop too. I know the SG called the White House. So, apparently, you've got some leverage. Something about your "heroic" performance." He laughed. "They don't know it, but that's just you being you. Brace yourself, you may be our new poster child."

"What?!? Buzzzzzzzzzz, wrong answer."

"Negatory, but of course I'm only speculating . . ."

"Alright, speculator, any other news I can use?"

"Ole ye Human again. . . "

"No theatrics."

"Killjoy. Okay. Reanders is in Santa Monica. I found that out by simple detective work and a tap into a local surveillance camera. You are the second person to know. Whatcha gonna do?"

"Could you send . . ." My message notification indicator beep.

"Done. Map too."

"Anything else I . . ." Indicator went off again.

"Your video went viral and someone put a soundtrack to it. Close-ups and everything. Enjoy." He hung up.

I walked back over to the Command Unit. Banner was talking to Richardson. They both looked my way.

Banner said, "You still in the know?"

I gave him a smile. "Now you will be, too. Any place secure to talk?"

"Yeah, the Command Unit."

He walked in and several people walked out after he said, "Folks."

Banner, Jim, Mary and I stepped in and he locked the door.

"That'll raise suspicions."

"My van. I get first dibs on debriefing. If Homeland wanted you so badly they should have approached you. Okay, give."

"Dr. Dorothy Reanders of the Reanders Institute is the creator of the variant Bath Salts and this new drug."

Richardson grunted. Banner listened. Jim and Mary looked at me. "She escaped NYPD custody

yesterday and we think with a high degree
of certainty she is here. She's a super genius
and very dangerous. We also think she's been
preparing for something like this for a while . . ."
Just then my cell went off. It was Cortez.

"Yeah?"

"Karen, transmission was through several
of the local Missions and food banks. She also
distributed free water and drinks to all the
homeless and locals. Only the needy would
accept."

"Thanks, Cortez. Can you send that to CDC?
In a meeting right now, but I'll call you later."

"Already Done. Vadnez is determined to have
our department get credit this time. Be good,
Girl." He hung up.

I looked at the group. "More news. The drug
was distributed through charitable means."

Banner said, "Makes sense. All of sudden help
swoops in from nowhere. What's our next move?
Or what's your next move?"

Indeed, what was my next move? "The FBI is
already after her, but they don't know where she
is. I have strong Intel that's possibly found her.
Sneaking up on her would be difficult. She was
able to remotely follow me through New York
City and effect the Traffic Lights on a whim. She

was also able to tap into my personal and official cell and momentarily disable them. To say she's terst is an understatement."

I thought for a few more seconds.

"She might even know we're on to her."

Jim said, "If sneaking up behind her won't work, how about knocking on her front door?"

Richardson said, "I'd like the LAPD to do the bust."

"I've no problems with that, but I need to confront her. If she even suspects a trap we'll lose her. We have some unfinished business and I left her pissed. I'll have to go alone. No wire, no electronics, just me."

Mary said, "She's the one who started all this?"

I nodded.

"That's crazy, Karen!"

"We can do this, we . . . "

"Not we, you. You're gonna be in there by yourself." Her eyes welled up with tears.

Banner said, "I got my money on you." He handed me his card. "Put me in contacts. Message me when or if you can and we'll be there in minutes."

Richardson looked at Jim, "Well, what do you want to do Officer?"

"Drive her there, sir. I can at least do that. Maybe wait nearby."

He nodded. "Alright then. If she's outside of LA I'll have to make a few phone calls."

"Santa Monica."

Richardson smiled. "Good, I know the chief over there. I can make this happen." He sat at his desk and took out his cell phone. A few button pushes later he was talking to someone. "Tanya! Me Frank. . . Peggy's good. So are the boys. . . How's Tom? . . . Good, good. . . So why the call? Glad you asked . . . remember how you always wanted a high profile takedown? . . . yes . . . yes . . . exactly . . ."

We left and let the Commander deal.

Once I stepped outside I was approached by Homeland Security. He flashed me his ID and said, "Homeland Security, Porter. Agent Karen Bechard?"

I flashed him mine. "That's me. How can I help you?"

"Someplace private?"

I smiled congenitally, "Most certainly." I turned to Mary and Jim. "Wait for me Guys. This hopefully won't be too long . . . " I looked Homeland in the eyes.

He said, "It shouldn't take long at all."

I followed him over to the Homeland Security Command Unit. We stepped inside.

Porter said, "Please have a seat, Agent Bechard. May I get you anything? We have Starbuck's coffee. Juice?"

"Coffee, please. No cream, no sugar."

He got it for me.

"Is there something you wanted to ask me?" I said sweetly and sipped my coffee. The temperature was perfect and the blend was yummy.

Mr. Porter relaxed.

"Not ask per se, but an offer."

"And that is?" I took another sip.

He said, "A job."

I nearly spat the coffee out. "A job?" Then I laughed. Porter joined me. "But I have a Job."

Porter said, "We know, but we would like to offer you a position within Homeland Security. It's a new division we're starting."

I sipped again, "I don't know what to say. What is this new division?"

"I can't give you many details yet, of course . . ." Porter said.

". . . of course."

"You would be in charge and would have

majority control of filling position."

"Majority?"

"There are some positions that would be reserved for promotion within. Some department heads within this division would be seeded with senior FBI staff. Some CIA. Some Military."

"Really? A multi-discipline division. Budget?"

"Main budget tied directly to the Pentagon. If you could justify an Ocean Liner you'd get it."

"R&D?"

"Ten percent from all branches."

Now that spoke volumes. Hidden research money. From all branches. Interesting. "You know I really like the UN. My boss, Vadnez, is pretty good to me."

Porter nodded. "He thinks very highly of you."

I almost spat that sip out, too.

"You've spoken to him?"

"Not me personally. The President, Homeland Security Secretary, your boss, and the UN Secretary General talked earlier."

He let that sink in.

"I'm gonna need more info."

Porter thought for a moment. "Homeland Security is a mishmash of departments. The 2008 act that created us left out the FBI and CIA. We did absorb some of their lesser departments but those were rather toothless. The Coast Guard gives us bite, but that is on the coast. So, by Executive Order a new department will be created."

"And by Executive Order it can be de-created."

"Agent Bechard . . . Agent Bechard, a job is something you never need worry about. In the US, in the UN, in anyplace. We . . . I am hoping I can arouse your curiosity enough to consider working for your home country. As director, you may not go out on many field mission, but you would have a major impact on those missions."

"And, that's the problem. I'm not a Director type. I don't think I ever will be . . . ."

He started to speak, but I held a finger up. "This is not to say I won't consider the position or one of those field positions. Can you give me a little more info?"

He thought several moments. "Please, keep this between us. The new division is a blend of FBI and CIA but under direct control of Homeland Security. Its jurisdiction is considerably wider than either of the two and you'd be working closely with the UN."

"My boss wants to talk to me after this is all

resolved. Can I give you an answer after that? Maybe do some serious talking?"

He knew he had me. He gave me a Cheshire cat grin. "Here's my card."

I stood up. "I'll give you my answer in a few days."

He stood up as well, "Of course." And walked me to the door.

Mary and Jim had been waiting outside. Before they could talk I said, "Everything is fine. I need a good bath." Off in the distance I could hear the sounds of machine gun fire. Victory through attrition, but with their side shrinking. We did most of the dirty work and they'll take the credit. I shrugged. C'est la vie.

Banner came up beside us. "Sucks pretty bad not to close one doesn't it?"

I nodded, "It's not going to be an easy close, but I would have liked to have finished."

"Well, there you go then. Job security." And he smiled.

"Banner," I said, "How would you like to be in the know? Often?"

He grunted, "Depends. How much of my soul will I have to sell?"

I smiled. "Not much really."

He said, "Now I should be afraid."

I gave him that punch to the shoulder again. "I'll give you a call later with more Intel."

He nodded, smiled.

Jim looked at me. "You got something cooking don't you?"

"I do." Then I turned and looked Jim in the eyes. "You ever think about something other than the LAPD?"

He nodded, "Yeah, I do, but I like my job."

"FBI, CIA?"

"Passing thoughts. But I suppose it would be nice working for the greater good. Local is good, but national is different. You get local and everything else."

"What about you, Mary? Thought about anything other than the airlines?"

Mary reflected some. "Sure I have. But being a flight attendant has lots of perks. Travel is free and I meet lots of interesting people." She looked me in the eyes. "Case in point."

I blushed. "But, if you had a choice. What career would you pick?"

"I got a charge out of shooting bad guys, but I know that's not the whole picture. I think I'd be too chicken to be a soldier or cop. Carrier maybe."

Jim asked, "Karen, why the questions?

Something with Homeland?"

I lied, "Not at all. I was just debriefing with Homeland. Richardson was right. If they had wanted me first they should have reached me first. Anyway, I was just curious. Really."

Banner looked me in the eyes and declared, "I'd never play poker with you."

We walked toward Jim's Truck. I handed him the keys. I asked Jim and Mary to give me a few minutes. I took out my cell, Mr. Porter's card, and dialed his number. A few seconds later we were talking.

"Mr. Porter, a question."

"Certainly, Agent Bechard. I'll answer as much as I can."

"I'm not the Director type. I'd wind up pissing folks off and making a mess of the whole thing. Pissing people off is what I do best. I'm more of a Field Operative. That's what I like and that would be the best place for me."

"Agent Bechard, Director Vadnez said as such. He also said you would turn down the Director position and ask for field operations instead."

Good old Vadnez. He does know me well.

"Suppose I gave you a recommendation for the Director position? How much pull do I have?"

"A lot."

"Okay, we can talk tomorrow morning?"

"Excellent. May I send a car to pick you up or would you rather drive to my office?"

"I'll drive there. Just message me the address and what's needed."

"Thank you, Agent Bechard. We have good days before and ahead of us."

I agreed and we hung up. I hopped into the truck and Jim drove Mary and myself to his apartment.

In the Truck I sent Cortez a message.

He replied, "Congratulations, Director Bechard."

I typed out "Topics

Thirty minutes later we pulled into Jim's parking spot. We dragged ourselves into his bedroom and promptly slept.

Voluntary or not, sit!

It was ten when we finally woke up. I turned on the TV and went straight to CNN. The military blew through the area and did a nice wrap up job. There was some collateral damage, but what would you expect. That was the military. The brute force arm of justice. Hammer against sewing pin. There was another segment on GI Jane and they wondered who I was. Lots of commentary from both Left and Right. Surprisingly, the Left applauded me for rescuing the family but thought my action excessive - since I was so skillful couldn't I have taken more arms and not as many heads? Some said charges should be pressed, those were people not in control. The Right felt I should have left the family, dealt with the problem and then went back to save them. A

CNN poll had favored my action by a good 73 points, which showed that those in position spoke what they thought and not what the people felt.

I switched the TV off and made breakfast for everyone. I wasn't sure about Mary's cooking but I knew Jim was an excellent chef. He was good at gourmet and I was good at the basics. I seasoned lightly, stuck to the staples. Jim was creative and made each home cooked dinner with me an event.

Minutes after I set the table Jim walked in. He kissed me hard. I said, "Nice to see you, too." I made pan scrambled eggs, toast, chopped mushrooms and chopped sausages. There was a plate waiting for him. He sat down and I poured him a screw driver.

Mary entered a few moments later and gave me a sweet kiss. I liked the way she tasted and wanted to go further but just returned the kiss just as sweet. She sat down. I had coffee in front of her plate.

I sat down after serving everyone.

And we ate. No talking, just eating. I had a bloody Mary with my meal.

When I poured Mary her second cup of coffee she said, "Karen, I'm afraid."

I said, "So am I, but I have to do this. I put myself in harm's way to help others, remember?"

Jim said, "But that doesn't mean we can't worry."

I nodded.

He said, "When do we do this?"

"Now. No need in letting this linger."

He nodded and Mary's eyes teared up again. She came over to me and gave me a big hug.

I said, "Seriously, I plan on coming out of this alive."

She said, "Promise?"

I nodded.

"Pinky promise?"

I gave her my pinky and we shook.

She smiled and kissed me again.

Sometime later I was standing in front of Reanders Institution. I knew she was in there. Cortez had snapped a photo of her near here. The FBI visited yesterday to investigate but had no evidence to permit a search. They did the standard interviews. Noted what they could and left. Me, on the other hand was different. All I had to do was stand in front of the building. A minute later a security guard came out.

I gave him my best smile.

He simply said, "Please follow me Miss."

I noticed he was high off of some substance

but couldn't tell what. He wasn't wasted, just super alert. Coffee could never do that.

He walked me through the gates, through the building, to a bank of elevators.

He inserted a key. We took an elevator to the top floor. Reanders was standing in front of us when the doors opened. She had three bodyguard types flanking her.

"Ms. Bechard, so nice to see you. How did you know?"

I walked in and the elevator door closed. It was me, Reanders, and her ghouls. They were on something. Their eyes were glassy but they were not Ragers. It was something different. "I have ways," and I smiled.

"No doubt. I'm still safe here, at least for the time being. Please join me," and she gestured to a chair.

"No brunch? No chitchat? Just right to business?"

She gestured again. "Voluntary or not."

I sat.

"Tie her up." She said.

Her guards duct taped my arms and legs to the chair.

She said, "I missed you, Karen. The last time we met had been under . . ." She thought

for a second. " . . . strenuous circumstances."
And laughed at her word choice. "We never
had a chance to just talk and enjoy each other's
company.

"True. You were running and I was chasing
you."

"Yes, but here we are."

She approached me and came within inches of
my face. Her eyes were intense. She hated me and
she wanted to do me in properly. "Karen, I'd have
to thank you. That stunt you pulled off back in
New York. It gave me firsthand experience."

"You're through business wise, you know
that?"

"Please. This is America. Money swings votes
and politicians need money. Half the Hawks in the
Senate and House would find a way to exploit my
new Military application. A few phone calls and
I'm under witness protection. Another few phone
calls and a dozen superpacs would be set for life.
You think the Kochs Brothers wield power in that
town? I got power."

"That includes kidnapping?"

She backed up. "It does. Phone call, charges
dropped." Then a thought hit her.

She came up real close and kissed me hard.
All of a sudden she became hypersexual. She

kissed my jawline and sucked hard along my neck, then it was over. She licked her lips and went back to the table.

"The side-effects of the drug is hypersexuality. I absorbed a great deal and the effects are just now wearing off. I think I'll make you my toy. Yeah, that would work splendidly. I created several variants. One rages the user. The second makes them hypersexual. The third makes them completely and utterly susceptible to suggestion. Given a few commands and you'll be my pet." She started laughing. "I so name thee Karen Mutt, my pet." And she laughed harder.

"Another added benefit is that the variants are not that highly addictive. The side-effects would be to some, but not the drug itself. The market potential alone would court billions of dollars to my behalf."

Sudden dread hit me. I was in over my head. The bad part was that I agreed with her. She'd have enough money to stay out of jail forever. She could pit politician against politician, government after government. I watched her as she worked and I noticed so did my guards. Several had hardons. I wondered how far this hypersexuality would go.

"Reanders, sorry."

She stopped working. "Pardon?"

"I'm sorry."

She took off her gloves and approached me cautiously. She looked me in the eyes with suspicious.

I looked away.

She smiled. "I'm preparing something especially potent for you."

"I don't think it'll be needed."

"My toy and my bodyguard. Perfect combo for you. It'll be needed alright. You're too much of a huntress to be trusted."

I leaned my head forward and pouted my lips.

She licked her's and kissed me again. I took her tongue and sucked on it passionately. She responded in kind. I don't know how long we kissed but it was long enough. She let go my jaw. "My toy" she whispered.

I said, "I want your other lips."

She kissed me again and didn't give any attention to her guards. She rubbed her breast against mine and dropped her hand between my legs. I was aroused so being wet came easy. She went down on me and licked hard. She moved my panties aside and bit down hard on my clit. Electric shock struck. She probed inside with a finger and sucked hard. Her aggressive touch set me off like never before. She then squeezed my clit and licked with fervor. I came within minutes. Strong intense waves, one after another. I was drained. She wiped her mouth and stood up. "My turn." She pulled her pants down and pulled her panties aside. She walked up to me and buried my face hard into her mound. She was rough and didn't give me a chance to use my tongue. She rubbed herself against my face harshly for minutes. Then she grabbed my ears and climaxed hard. Her legs quivered violently at each convulsion. When she finished she pulled her pants back up and said, "Now wasn't that nice?" She turned back to the table. "That was a very nice diversion."

I said, "What about them?"

"Who? My guards?"

They all had raging hardons.

She looked and giggled. "I should let them rape you, but you'd be no good after that."

"How about you fuck them."

She thought about that.

I looked at one of them, "You liked that didn't you. How I came on her face and I how she face fucked me. Turned you on didn't it."

Realization set on her face as she saw things to come.

"She likes it in the ass, you know. She likes it rough. You could come on . . ."

She screamed, "Shut up" and slapped me.

" . . . You can come all over her nice pretty pale ass and that lovely face of her's."

She hit me again and tried to choke me.

I started to blackout when suddenly her hands were gone. She screamed as the guards grabbed her. One yanked her glasses off her face and tossed them. He tore her lab coat off and ripped her shirt open. A second one pulled her pants halfway down. He thrusted hard and started pumping. Her cries were muffled as the first one grabbed her jaw and made her suck. The third guard was jerking off and watching. He was waiting for his turn. I said, "Untie me and I'll fight back too."

That did it. He ripped the duct tape off my arms and legs. I throat chopped him before he had other ideas. His windpipe caved in.

Reanders screamed and struggled. I walked over to my purse, pulled out my cell and messaged Banner. "Ready, but Guard at gate might be a problem. He has key to Express elevator." Then I placed a 911 call and reported a rape in progress at the Reanders Institute. Minutes later Banner and his men arrived, with Santa

Monica PD behind. Jim entered seconds later holding his badge. SWAT stepped out the elevator and took the two guards down. Apparently, the variant Reanders used didn't Rage them and so they had near normal strength.

Reanders laid on the floor sobbing and shaking. There was blood between her legs and I gave no pity.

I composed myself and straightened my panties. I brushed my dress clean and took the elevator to the lobby. Jim was next to me but didn't say a word. Santa Monica PD made the arrest. A minute later, two EMTs with a stretcher walked in. An FBI agent followed. A few minutes after that they all came out. Reanders was tied down. As they were passing, Reanders said, "Please stop. I want to say a few things to Ms. Bechard." They stopped.

I looked her in the eyes.

Her stare was focused and intense. They were the clearest I've seen. "Ms. Bechard, 'I am leaving you with a gift—peace of mind and heart. And the peace I give is a gift the world cannot give. So don't be troubled or afraid.'"

I didn't respond, but I didn't let her see fear. We stared at one another for a few more seconds. Then she said, "Okay, I am done. Take me away."

The truth was, I was afraid. One part scary-genius, one part rage, result is sometime dangerous. I still had the satisfaction in knowing that a bullet to the head would solve everyone's problem. We continued to stare at one another. Just before they lifted her into the ambulance I outstretched my arm and held my hand in a gun pose. I snapped my thumb down in a double tap.

She understood and that was all I needed.

After the ambulance pulled away I made a call to Vadnez. He told me no need to head back to the office so soon. All transfer paperwork would be handled promptly. I could do a video conference with him and the SG in the morning from Mr. Porter's office.

When I called Mr. Porter he had been expecting my call. He said we could work out the details tomorrow morning and I'd get a full disclosure on what the positions entailed. I gave him my Director recommendation. He said very well and he would take care of the rest. A few minutes later Banner's cell went off. I was watching him when he answered. After about five minutes he hung up and walked over to me.

He had a questioning look on his face.

I smiled and said, "If they like you and you

like them you'll be in the know. Really in the know."

He laughed and gave me a light punch to the shoulder. Jim and Mary I would tell later. This evening I was going to relax and be merry. Then I remembered Casper Schenk's Farewell to Grog song. And thought out the first verse:

> Come, messmates, pass the bottle 'round
> Our time is short, remember,
> For our grog must stop,
> And our spirits drop,
> On the first day of September.
> For tonight we'll merry, merry be,
> For tonight we'll merry, merry be,
> For tonight we'll merry, merry be,
> Tomorrow we'll be sober.

The End

RAGE

ABOUT THE AUTHOR

J Carrell Jones studies people. His major in college was Anthropology before switching over to Computer Science and Information Technology. He worked in the Customer Support Services for many years, which gave him more opportunity in putting his understanding about people to good practical use. As a US Army veteran, he knows how to play hard and work tough. Nowadays, he gets his greatest joys in life by raising his brilliant young daughter, and writing.He lives in Southern California where the weather is mostly great with his wife, daughter, female cat, and three female Guinea pigs.

132